THE SCIENCE OF DRAGONS

JULIE KRAMER

The Science of Dragons © January 2018 by Julie Kramer

Acknowledgments

My thanks, in no particular order: To my family, for providing inspiration and encouragement

(And for listening to me rant)

To my first readers, for helping me iron out the kinks.

To everyone that has influenced this book.

And to you, my reader. Thank you for being a part of this journey with me. I wish you all the blessings that life has to offer.

Chapter One

B linding pain erupted in my right shoulder, searing like a blazing fire. I lay sprawled on the ice, panting softly and praying that the biting coolness against the back of my jersey would soothe the ache; no such luck. I closed my eyes briefly, listening to the scritch-scratch of skates on ice and feeling the tiny shavings of ice land on my jersey as the team skidded to a halt next to me. There was a shuffling sound, and I opened my eyes to see several faces of my teams arrayed above me. Ash was nearest. He touched my shoulder gently with his long fingers and correctly interpreted the soft noise I made as a pained wince.

"Are you okay?" he asked worriedly. When I didn't answer, his hand tightened on my bicep, making me gasp as pain shot through my side, from below my ribcage, through my collarbone and to the point of my shoulder. He let go immediately. I knew he hadn't meant to hurt me, so I didn't hold it against him.

"Alex?" Despite the agony, I nodded and mumbled a yes, breathing shallowly through my teeth as I tried and failed to sit up. That wasn't good enough for Coach, who shoved through the pile and knelt next to Ash.

"Does it hurt anywhere?" he demanded, the tone of his deep, scraping voice warning me not to lie. I sighed quietly and pointed at my shoulder. I had been caught out in lies before about what hurt and how badly, and the last time had ended with me in the hospital. I hoped never to repeat the experience.

Ash helped me up and off the ice, his large, slender hands surprisingly gentle, fending off the rest of the worried team with sharp elbows and furiously whispered threats. They backed off, leaving reluctantly when Coach barked, "Go home!" Rather than shoving and jostling to exit the rink through the narrow opening like they usually did, they scooted back and allowed me to squeeze through first, supported by Ash. I smiled gratefully and waved him off as soon as we reached my dressing room, tugging my jersey carefully over my head with one hand. Ash flushed and turned away, which had been my plan. Well-meaning as he was, he probably would have followed me in if I hadn't done that. I closed the door behind me and wiggled the lock back and forth, the creased wood around the latch making it difficult to flip. I dug through my duffel bag, slowing each time a too-sudden motion jolted my shoulder. It thumped like a second heart, each burst a jagged reminder of my latest foolishness. I sank down on the stool and wriggled into the first clean tee shirt I found in my bag, which happened to be a concert tee for a band that had stopped touring before I was even born. My mother hated it, but it was comfortable. Standing, I ducked as my sudden proximity to a bar reminded me that there was an obstacle there. This closet had only ever been used as a supply closet, but as the only female hockey player at our school, I couldn't exactly be expected to change with the boys. You would think that as often as I used this tiny little room, I would realize that the bar was right there, especially after the first time I'd come home from practice with a bruise on my cheekbone that had nothing to do with hockey. No such luck, but I ducked carefully under the bar as I tugged my royal blue varsity jacket on, the crossed hockey sticks on the upper arm standing out vividly against the black sleeve. My shoulder let loose with a brief stab of pain. That's going to hurt in the morning, I thought blithely.

I shoved out of the rink doors and trudged toward home, not paying any particular attention to my surroundings until I noticed a nondescript black sedan at the edge of my peripheral vision. The windows were tinted far darker than was legal, but I still caught a flash of pale blue, a sway of inky black. A sudden, completely out of the blue thought occurred to me: They're following me. As soon as I thought it, I chided myself for being paranoid. Just because there was a car within a block of me, that didn't mean that they were following me. Still, I couldn't shake this prickly feeling in my stomach, although it wasn't a bad feeling, per se, which was odd.

I lengthened my already long strides, staring stubbornly ahead at a row of drab brown trash cans. My feet ached along with my shoulder, which gave me an excuse to glare at them rather than at the ugly trash cans.

I jerked hard and craned my head to glance over my shoulder when I heard the abrupt squeal of tires. The sedan had vanished with that slightly suspicious screech, so quickly I could smell the burnt rubber and see the dark tire treads ingrained onto the road. I had almost managed to convince myself that they weren't following me, but now I wasn't so sure.

I shook my head wryly, chiding myself again. One too many knocks to the head today. One of my earnest, but not-genius, teammates had body-checked me into the rink hall, hard.

I made it to my driveway without incident. Lost in thought, the toe of my black-and-turquoise high tops caught a loose pebble and I nearly fell on my face. Oh, the bitter irony. An hour and a half on slick ice and I nearly wiped out in my own driveway.

I fumbled with the silver key ring clipped to my duffel bag, sifting through them until finally peeling away the jagged silver key with a rounded head. I inserted it and twisted, hearing a subtle click as I shoved the door open. I stepped over the threshold into an empty house, like I did every day. I kicked the door shut behind me with my heel, then flipped the deadbolt with my thumb. Maybe I was being overly paranoid, thinking that the sedan may have been following me, possibly even to my home, but nobody ever died from being too cautious. My nerves were already on the edge of a fine-toothed comb, and the last thing I needed was for something to happen while I was home alone with an injured shoulder. I hurled my duffel bag halfway up the stairs with my good arm so that I didn't accidentally trip over it. It landed in the middle of a step with a satisfying thump and promptly fell back down the stairs to fall at my feet. I stared at it in disgust, then shrugged and stepped over it, not bothering to try again.

Plucking a red apple from the bowl in the center of the kitchen table and taking a big, juicy bite out of the slippery crimson skin, I read the post-it note pasted on the refrigerator door. Unlike most homes, our fridge didn't have anything personal on it except a range of post-it notes in various different colors. There were no magnets or pictures of any kind, because my mom hated anything superfluous. It drove her bonkers when I left anything lying around, so I didn't do it unless I was itching for a fight. The three people who occupied our house were almost never in it at the same time, due to my parents' irregular work schedules. The only reason that the post-it notes were allowed to be on there was since, in our house, putting one of those on there was the equivalent of taking out a full page ad in the newspaper that said, "Look here! Underwear!" or something equally scandalous that was guaranteed to grab your attention.

Somehow my mother and my father, both doctors, had found out that I had injured my shoulder. The note, which practically oozed with my mother's bossy tone, ordered me to wear the sling they had sent home; it lay on the counter, daring me to disobey my mother and face the consequences. Between the two of them, neither of their specialties were anything near arm-related. I wasn't sure where they got their expertise in telling me to wear the most complicated sling I had ever seen. And believe me, I've seen my fair share of slings. And casts, braces, splints, and... I had some sort of experience with practically everything injury-related.

I growled, racking my brain in an attempt to figure out exactly how my parents had found out. They were both in the middle of a double shift at the hospital that wouldn't be over until well into the night, so they shouldn't have known about about it for quite a while longer. Unless... Mrs. Trist, the school nurse, must have called them at work to tattle on me and get brownie points, not that it would have worked. My parents hated her; they knew what she was all about. Not to mention that she wouldn't know a proper diagnosis if it bit her in the keister. Now I'd have to wear the stupid sling. I stared at it, trying to decide if it was worth it to try to put it on right now. My mom always said that if you don't listen to the doctor, it'll just hurt worse, but honestly, I got hurt so often it didn't really matter anymore. Tomorrow, however, was a very different story. Someone would notice it, everyone would ask about it, and in the following three seconds I would be benched. And there wasn't a single thing I could do about it.

With a frustrated groan, I stalked up the carpeted stairs and into the bathroom, snagging a towel and my thick terry robe on the fly. The partially eaten apple sailed into my trash can, a perfect shot, the remnant of my years on the basketball team before the drama pushed me into hockey. I swept down and snatched up the pair of pale purple slippers laid next to the twin bed before closing the blinds and flipping on the squat space heater already plugged in. My parents kept the house freezing cold, which made getting out of a hot shower an especially unpleasant experience. A long shower would ease my mind; or possibly, my shoulder.

Chapter Two

I slid sideways into my desk just as the bell rang, panting softly. Coach had been on the warpath this morning when he'd seen the sling. It wrapped around my stomach and over my shoulder to hold my arm in place. It wasn't even that bad, as I had tried, unsuccessfully, to convince both Coach and Ash, but no one ever listens to me. As I'd expected, I was benched for an indefinite amount of time. I also had to clear any further participation with at least one of my parents, or another doctor, before I could come back. I wanted to talk to my parents as much as any other teenager, i.e., not at all. My mother would be a joy to deal with, because she hadn't wanted me to play hockey in the first place, saying it was unladylike. Like I cared about that, but it didn't help that she now had another injury, joining the many others, to hold over my head.

Halfway through my third class, a soft knock rang out in the otherwise silent classroom. The teacher glanced up from his crossword puzzle, his bushy white eyebrows shooting toward the sky. I glanced up from my worksheet as a boy stepped over the threshold. In an epic moment of gracelessness, he promptly tripped on his own shoe and tumbled forward, his possessions flying out of his grip. He flushed bright red, even on the tips of his ears and the back of his neck. I slid out of my desk and strode over to join him, wincing as my knees cracked audibly when I crouched next to him. My injured arm made it difficult to balance in such an awkward position, so I lowered myself to my knees on the floor and reached to help him stack his belongings in a neat pile. He stood first and offered me a hand up, which I accepted gratefully. His long fingers wrapped gently around the back of my hand for a better grip, and he held on for a moment too long, just long enough for the teacher to clear his throat. I thanked him quietly at the exact moment that he thanked me, which made us both grin. He slipped into an unoccupied desk catty-corner to mine after carefully balancing the reassembled stack on the flat top, his long body slouching bonelessly, like he was trying to melt into the scratched tile. The teacher gave him no reprieve.

"Why don't you stand up and introduce yourself?" he hinted. The boy unfolded slowly to his full height, broad shoulders hunched, and stared at the nondescript colored tile between his feet.

"Meisha Anix," he mumbled shyly, staring down and scuffing at a black mark on the tile with his shoe. His desk squealed embarrassingly as he tilted back into it like a falling tower, leaning heavily on the shiny metal side bar. The teacher bent over the new boy's desk and dropped a paper onto its surface, pointing with one knobby finger and speaking in low, uninterested tones. Apathy radiated from his watery brown eyes.

I was ambidextrous, so it wasn't too hard for me to write with my left hand, although it took some concentration. I tried my best, but I found myself distracted by the new boy, Meisha. It was very strange that there were two new boys in such a short amount of time, when most of the time there were years between new students, especially such attractive ones. I studied him covertly, pretending to solve a problem but really completely ignoring the complex problems on my worksheet, trying to decide whether he was pretty or simply hot. He had a very slim face and body, which lent itself to pretty, but everything else was masculinely attractive. He had lush, extremely dark brown hair, hypnotizing, long lashed blue-purple eyes, and tanned skin that suggested he spent a lot of time outside. His neck and face were windburned; maybe he spent time at high altitudes? A climber, maybe? His strong, callused hands supported that theory. He stuttered slightly when he spoke, but I was pretty sure it was only nervousness, rather than a speech impediment.

The piercing shriek of the bell that told us to switch classes rang out, startling me out of my stupor. Poor Meisha looked like he was going to faint from relief. He dove for his books, then slapped his palm lightly on the top of the stack in frustration when he realized he had no idea where he was supposed to go. I glanced at him briefly but didn't stop, juggling my books impatiently when I reached the crush at the door. The way he looked, he'd have a flock of girls lining up to be his guide. I was still waiting to be let out from the crush at the door when the teacher called me back. I sighed darkly and retreated, racking my brain for anything that I had or hadn't done. Like my day wasn't bad enough already. I didn't have time for this. It would take me too long to finagle my things into my locker with an injured arm as it was. Whatever this was would only make me even later.

I strode toward the teacher's desk, slowing my strides when Meisha shifted. I knew what I looked like: at just over six feet tall, with the broad shoulders and defined muscle tone of an athlete, I was striking to say the least. I wasn't surprised that he was a little wary, because I could be fierce. Especially if I was angry. I wasn't angry yet, just curious and somewhat resigned, but it wouldn't be too far of a leap to get there. All it would take was if whatever this little escapade was made me late for my next class, late enough to get into trouble. I wasn't against a little rebellion now and then, but I was already on thin ice with my parents, and I couldn't afford to dig myself an even deeper hole.

"Can you show Meisha to his next class?" the teacher asked. Judging by Meisha's pained wince, the pronunciation of his unique name had just been thoroughly butchered. He had pronounced it like May-cha, whereas when Meisha himself had done it earlier in class, it had been more like My-sha.

I stared for a second, stunned at whatever irony had decreed that I, probably the only girl around who *didn't* want to be the hot boy's guide, had been elected for the position. A gaggle of them stood in the doorway of the room across the hall, in fact, watching like predators but batting their long eyelashes when he glanced in their direction. If looks could kill, they'd have been digging my grave and sayin' the sermon. I shook myself and walked away with a curt nod, not caring whether or not he followed me. He did, shoes scuffing as he stumbled.

"What's your next class?" I asked without stopping. Our lockers were quite a walk from here. We were irreversibly late, but I still had to switch out my books if I didn't want to make the trip again in the middle of class when I needed them. He fumbled for his schedule; there was a muffled word that made me raise my brows before he pushed the brightly highlighted page over my shoulder. I took it and scanned for the room number and teacher. "Calculus." The class that I had next, which was just as well, since I didn't really feel like going out of my way. He followed me like a lost puppy, and I resigned myself to the long day ahead.

Considering Meisha was in every one of my classes, it made it difficult to, well, I wasn't sure. I wanted to dislike him for the inconvenience and the fact that I genuinely wasn't in a very good mood that day, but I couldn't. He was extremely polite and asked minimal questions, his strange black-ringed eyes taking everything in like a sponge. The only strike against him was that he was so attractive, which didn't make much sense. He was the only one who didn't seem to notice; every girl around did, though. They crowded around, their obnoxious giggles so high-pitched that I was surprised bats didn't come swooping in, searching for kindred spirits. Each screeching titter exponentially increased the chance that I was gonna hit someone before the day ended. Possibly with a hockey stick. And I wasn't going to be sorry.

Meisha and I were on our way to chemistry, our last class of the day, when we were waylaid. The door to the high school office, a large glass cubicle that was less of a fish bowl and more of a terrarium, swung wide to reveal a very bored secretary. She waved us in, chomping her gum. *Oh, no*, I thought grimly. *If she pops that gum, I may kill her.* I was wound too tightly to deal with this right now.

She wore a zebra print pencil skirt, paired with a lime green, ruffled top that made her look like a pirate. Even with my limited fashion knowledge, I knew that was a distinct faux pas. Her zebra print flats, the only thing in that forsaken outfit that actually coordinated, clicked on the Plexiglas mat behind her desk.

The rude secretary informed me that someone wanted to speak with me, but I would have to wait. I opened my mouth to point out that Meisha needed someone to guide him, but she had already returned to chatting on the phone. Her chubby sausage fingers twisted the cord, making me think that she was probably gossiping. I fumed, but even with largely absent parents I wasn't rude enough to march up to her, yank the phone out of her hand, and tell her to think about why someone she hadn't called in had followed me. My bad mood dissipated when said follower leaned over to whisper in my ear, his voice low and silky. "I don't mind missing class."

Before I could respond, an unfamiliar man stepped out of the nearest office. I'd expected school staff to be old, balding, have bad teeth, and wear a cheap suit. None of the above. He wore faded jeans, an obscure band t-shirt, with sandy blond hair that flopped over jewel blue eyes. Talk about an expectation breaker.

To my confusion, the man marched over to Meisha, who'd shifted to a chair nearer to the glass so he could observe the passerby, and started talking to him like he was an old friend. He gestured animatedly: at me, the office he'd just left, the rude secretary. Meisha nodded or shook his head, speaking in undertones, clearly answering questions. The man nodded when he finished. He loped over to the secretary, who punched what I assumed was the hold button and put down her phone for the first time since we'd walked in. He leaned over the desk to speak with her, and she fluttered her hands and batted her lashes while he spoke. *Probably not used to speaking with attractive men*, I thought uncharitably. Finished with his conversation, the man straightened up and waved at Meisha, then pulled the heavy glass door open and left.

Apparently wires were crossed somewhere along the line, because no one actually wanted to speak with me. Meisha left when school dismissed, throwing me an apologetic glance over his shoulder. The secretary kicked me out, and I was headed for the door before she finished her sentence. I stopped by my locker to grab my work, heaving my hefty textbooks into my bag, and stalked toward the doors to begin the long walk home.

The school was eerie with half of the motion sensor lights out, rippling on in front of me like a cresting ocean wave and then dropping off behind me, clipping my heels with the darkness. I lengthened my strides and tried not to look to either side of me, where class and individual pictures hung, from ancient, water stained circles of women with bulky hairstyles and frumpy dresses all the way through present day with carefully coiffed hair and bright grins. I was a senior, so my picture would be up here after graduation, entombed behind clear glass until it was just as out of date as the men with the weird ponytails and cravats or whatever the flip they were called. I hitched my bag higher on my shoulder, feeling the books shift within, and sighing when I realized how badly my already unorganized pile would look when I opened it.

I turned the corner and ran into someone - literally. A spike of pain jolted through my injured arm and I yelped, folding in half to press it against my stomach. A face appeared as someone crouched in front of me. His eyes were a startling, bright blue, his black bangs so long that they tangled in the lush lashes until he tossed his head. I tried to breathe evenly as pain radiated through my arm. The boy's face was worried and contrite.

"I'm so sorry," he breathed. "I didn't even see you." He laid his hand gently on my arm but didn't press, offering support whenever I was ready. I straightened up slowly and he removed his hand as soon as he was sure that I was alright. My breathing had steadied, but I couldn't look at him. Of course I had managed to run into the most attractive guy in the building, with wild black hair and piercing, royal blue eyes. Just my luck; not that I was complaining.

"It's fine," I mumbled. "Excuse me." I brushed past him and walked away as quickly as I could. The shuffle of shoes made it sound like he'd turned to watch me go, but there were no accompanying footsteps, for which I was grateful. Hopefully, I would see him tomorrow during school hours and we could have a proper meeting, hopefully without any mention of this particular incident. I headed for home, and touched my arm gently where his hand had rested. I couldn't stop the grin that crept onto my lips, and the hope that I would see him again.

Chapter Three

An unfamiliar black sedan crouched imposingly in my driveway. I briefly entertained the thought of skirting around, climbing up the rowan tree in the backyard to reach my balcony, grabbing my hockey stick, and braining anyone inside. Good plan, except with only one good arm, I was more likely to fall out of the tree and take the other one out of commission. Either that, or I'd get stuck like a treed raccoon.

My parents, both influential doctors, worked all the time. As a result, nearly every summer when I was younger they'd dumped me at summer camps. The dancing one hadn't been worth the ridiculously bright pink paper the pamphlet was printed on, but the climbing had been fun, and useful.

I crept up my driveway, onto my porch, and through my unlocked front door. Three adults sat inside, deep in conversation. Meisha sat on the edge of the smallest chair, looking mortally, fatally bored.

I dropped my duffel bag on the hardwood floor as loudly as I could, hoping to startle an explanation out of the group. My mother looked kid-in-a-candy-store excited, which in itself made me wary. Nothing that made her that excited could be any good for me. I plopped down on the only empty chair, my comfy leather recliner, and tried to scoot forward subtly to the edge. I crossed my legs, because my mom hated it when I was "unladylike" and I wasn't ready to make her mad just yet, not before I figured out what was going on. The vaguely familiar man shot a look at my parents and cleared his throat.

"My name is Chase Fernis. I work for a private program that would like to offer your daughter a place with us. We think she'd be an excellent addition, but we have limited places available." He spoke directly to my parents, which ticked me off. If I was the one being offered a position, why was he talking to them?

"What kind of program?" I asked curiously. He wrinkled his nose.

"I'm afraid I'm not at liberty to share that information at this time," he said, in that obnoxious tone adults use to address kids when they're trying to get rid of them, which ticked me off. I was sixteen, not six. He turned back to my parents, a clear snub. "You'll learn more after your parents decide.

"Of course we have an excellent schooling regimen," he continued. "She'd still get a wonderful education, along with other real life skills you won't find anywhere else."

He just sounds pompous now, I thought darkly. My jaw hit the floor when my mother spoke, and I wouldn't have been surprised if there had been a clunk like a dropped anvil in a cartoon.

"Why don't you head up to your room?" my mom suggested dismissively. "Leave the adults to speak privately."

I was breathless with rage, but my mind cleared like someone had wiped a slate.

"Sure," I said casually. "If Meisha comes." I loped up the stairs, anticipating Meisha would follow me, which he did. He skirted a bit too far around my dad's chair; I found it hilarious. The only fight my dad had ever been in, he'd slapped his opponent in the face with a dish towel. Not exactly fight club material.

I ambushed Meisha in my room as he closed the door. He knew more than me, which was not okay right now. He glanced around my room curiously. I could only imagine what he was seeing. My room was relatively tame compared to others I had seen, an odd mix of hockey paraphernalia and the girly things my mother foisted on me. The elegant rose patterned wall paper was covered with posters of famous hockey players, wooden racks adorned with medals and trophies, and crossed hockey sticks, along with a cork message board. Pamphlets and flyers for colleges across the country were tacked up, those same tacks poked into a large map. Meisha seemed fascinated with all the tiny things that made my room mine. I gestured for him to take a seat on the fluffy quilt covering my bed and pulled out my desk chair, my long legs stretching to the sides to straddle it.

I settled myself on the round seat and took a minute to run through my options. What was the best way to go about getting the information I wanted from him?

"What's he talking about?" I asked, deciding the simplest approach was probably best.

He hesitated, refusing to meet my eyes. "You'll know soon enough." His long brown hair slithered over one eye as he tilted his head, studying my purple shag carpeting like it held the secrets of the universe. My mother loathed this carpet with the burning passion of a thousand suns, but when it was the only thing I had asked for as a birthday present, she'd had no choice but to relent. I had a sneaking suspicion that my father had played a large role in that particular decision.

I dismissed his dull answer with an airy wave of my hand, pressing my chest against the soft back pad.

"Not good enough."

He spread his hands helplessly. "I can't tell you anything. All I can say is that you should probably start packing. It'll save you some time."

I glared. "It's not over yet. They could still say no."

"Yes," he conceded, tapping his long fingers on his knee. A ring glittered on one of his fingers, shining silver. "But Chase is very persuasive. Plus, free, elite education, and…"

"And the chance to get rid of me," I finished. He flushed in embarrassment and nodded sheepishly, raising his broad shoulder in a shrug. His long fingers ceased tapping on his jeans and began twisting the silver ring on his right ring finger, an aged silver beauty that looked very old and expensive. Another ring rested above it on the same finger, a sleek titanium number. It suddenly struck me that this boy wore more jewelry than I did, even when forced to wear the ugly pearl strands that my mother insisted on. She was lucky if I wore anything in the holes in my ears other than small diamond studs. Even that much didn't feel worth the effort most days.

I glared at Meisha for a moment before I kicked out of my chair, yanked open the door and stormed out of my room. My footsteps echoed as I stalked down the carpeted stairs. When I arrived, the conversation was just finishing. My parents zeroed in on me like a dog on a Frisbee; I braced for the worst.

"You're going," my mother announced. I couldn't believe my ears.

"I'm sorry, say *what* now?!"

My father threw an irritated look at her, which must have made her realize this wasn't the best way to go about telling me. She ignored him and continued, her dainty, aristocratic mouth pulling up to curl her lip at my gall, like she couldn't believe that I dared to question her. I did.

"Your father and I have talked it over. This is a great opportunity for you. This is for your own good," she soothed. Another look from my father, like, *Don't bring me into this*. That same look had been at the root of most of my childhood. When my mother said no to me, which was any time I wanted something she didn't consider "appropriate", I had gone running to my father. The decision didn't always change, but sometimes it did. That fact prompted me to turn to my father, hoping my face portrayed the range of emotions I was cycling through. Mostly anger, with a little panic and indignance mixed into the cocktail.

"What about school?" I protested. "Hockey?"

"Chase will take care of everything," she promised. "Get you transferred, do the paperwork. You leave in two days."

"You're not listening to me!" I raged. My fists clenched so tightly that my short, clipped nails dug crescents into the tender skin of my palm, skin stretched tight and white across my bony knuckles.

My mother fixed me with a withering look, not at all a match to the simpering smile on her lips. My dad opened his mouth to speak, but even he seemed reluctant to get in front of the train that was pulling away. "You will not speak to me that way," she hissed, her voice deathly quiet. "Especially not in front of our guests."

I seethed, breathless with fury, unsure of what to say. My mother was not the sort you argued with; that's how she'd gotten where she was. One doesn't become a prominent female doctor, on the verge of great positions at any hospital she wanted, without pushing back at anyone who pushed her. My father genuinely loved what he did, whereas my mother was all ambition. I was terrified of becoming her, which is one of the reasons I played hockey. In high school, she'd been a cheerleader, track and cross country runner. Despite her hectic schedule and the drama that came with school sports, her academics never suffered. She graduated top of her class in both high school and college, while I was an average student. I was the most tomboyish, bookish child you could have imagined, a walking, talking contradiction. She never missed a chance to mold me in her image, not that it was going too well so far.

"Fine," I snarled. "I'll leave the 'adults' to talk." I all but air-quoted the words, pouring every bit of my teenage sarcasm into them. My father might hear out my side of the story, if I could get him away from my mother, but she never would.

Chase bowed out gracefully. My mother was, as ever, the perfect hostess, thanking him for visiting and attempting to convince him to stay. He was just as deft, shaking his head gently and politely refusing. I saw Meisha, who had followed me down, wave shyly. I was too busy glaring at my mother to respond as he stepped out.

I spun on my heel and marched up the stairs two at a time, slamming my bedroom door with all my strength, which was formidable. The door jamb squeaked a protest as the lock clicked into place. "I'm not going!" I shouted at the top of my lungs.

Boy, was I wrong. Had I known then what I know now, I would have packed my bags and been waiting in the car with the keys in the ignition. But I didn't.

Chapter Four

Over the course of the next two days, I threw the biggest fit of my life. I pleaded, shouted, and threatened, to no avail. My mother headed me off at every turn while my father watched and tried to do damage control.

I staunchly refused to pack, so she did it for me, far more neatly than I could ever have managed, immaculate rows of clothing and other necessities tucked into a luggage set that was a near perfect match to my atrocious wallpaper. I would have unpacked it if she hadn't hidden it in the downstairs closet, secured by a simple key padlock. Had I particularly wanted to, I could have picked it, but that wasn't a skill I cared to reveal yet. I'd learned it during my long months of hanging out with a less than savory crowd for attention. When my parents either didn't notice or simply didn't care, I'd left of my own volition. I had nothing more to gain from hanging out with them. Besides, they weren't my crowd. Stick me in a room with athletes, I'll mingle and make friends with minimal effort. Ditto a room with readers. With the troublemakers, that's where I had, well, trouble. I just wasn't that kind of person.

I felt a perverse sense of satisfaction when I saw her expression as she walked into my room. My room was typically filthy, but being cooped up in here in a bad mood definitely hadn't improved it. Clothes were strewn everywhere; my CDs, typically inserted neatly into a rotating tower, glittered in a silver pile on my bed from when I had tried in vain to find one to listen to. The lid on my CD player was flipped up, gaping open accusingly. She ordered me to clean it up, but her defeated expression told me she knew what I did: it was not going to happen.

I wouldn't eat, so my mom did the mean thing: she cooked my favorite meal (fettuccine alfredo) and left it out, even waving the tantalizing scent up the stairs so that it wafted up to me. No go. I waited stubbornly in my room, flopped on my bed with 80s rock music blasting in my eardrums. Or so she thought. As a matter of fact, my dad, the softie, smuggled a bowl up while she was in the shower. I wolfed it down in huge bites and hurried back downstairs, where my father was elbow deep in white soap suds. We had a dishwasher, which I pointed out, but he winked and took my bowl from my hands. We washed the evidence and put it away before she was any the wiser.

I refused to do my chores, so my poor dad got stuck with them. I watched him take out the trash, mow the lawn, and weed-whack. My mother weeded the garden, but only to seem more domestic. She would wave and smile, the perfect picture of a trophy wife. Her lush, pin-straight blond hair and icy blue eyes were a vast ocean away from my wavy, light brown locks and black-ringed green eyes. I looked nothing like my father, either; his curly blonde hair made him look like an angel, even with thick glasses obscuring his blue eyes, faded like a favorite pair of jeans.

Late the night before I was to leave, I did what most teenagers would do when presented with a sketchy person who has the potential to vastly change their life: I searched the Internet for them. I looked for Chase Fernis all over the Internet, on social media, chat rooms, forums. I cyberstalked him, basically, with nothing to show for it. He was nowhere to be found. I couldn't find any mention of him anywhere, not even when I ran background checks on him.

My mother scared the bejeezus out of me when she strode into my room late on that last night, interrupting a hockey game on my laptop. I clicked pause and sat up cautiously, tugging my ear buds out one at a time. She was carrying a massive black file box that dwarfed her slender frame. I could hear her huffing and puffing, but by the time I had taken pity on her and stood to help, she had already plopped it down on the end of my bed, which tilted alarmingly in that direction. She went to sit on the other side, which helped to even out the weight distribution just a little bit. A mushroom cloud of dust bloomed as she pulled off the lid to the box, and I sneezed violently. She knew that I had allergies, but I had a feeling that wasn't why she had come.

"I know you think I'm being too harsh," she began. I raised an eyebrow and waited for her to continue. "But I want you to know why I'm doing this. I know we haven't always been very close, and I thought it was time to change that."

"A little late, don't you think?" I pointed out acerbically. She blanched slightly, which was the first time in a long time that I had seen her display any sign of weakness or compromise. Without another word, she reached into the box and handed a piece of paper to me. I skimmed it; my eyes widened when I saw the number at the bottom. She nodded.

"That's how much we pay, per semester, to send you to the most elite private school in the area. Now, don't get me wrong, we're proud of you. So proud, but..." She took a deep breath. "There's something we haven't told you."

"What are you talking about?"

She took a deep breath. "We didn't want to worry you, but... the hospital has been having trouble. Your dad and I have been trying to pick up the slack, but there's only so much that we can do. There's talk of them closing down, and if that happens, we'll have to move somewhere else. That's why this opportunity is such a blessing. This way, our money troubles will be much less, but you will still have all the opportunities we wanted to give you."

There was a lump in my throat, and I tried to swallow it. It was like trying to swallow a wad of chalk. "Why didn't you tell me? I would have moved schools, gotten a job, something."

She scooted forward an inch, holding her arms wide, her eyes questioning. I smiled briefly and scooted into her arms, hugging her tightly. I still wasn't happy about it, but I understood her insistence that I do this now.

I had tried everything I could think of, and I still wasn't happy with the situation, but I had sort of resigned myself to it. Chase and Meisha had been nowhere to be found since they had left my house a few days ago; I would have been worried if I hadn't been so ticked. Neither had the seriously attractive black-haired boy, which I was a bit sad about. On my last day to school, I strode into homeroom, juggling my open backpack with books in the other hand. In another small rebellion against my mother, I'd refused to organize my bag at home like I'd been told; I was regretting it now. I'd have to go through it here and hope I didn't miss anything. Though I considered "missing" the one library book I had checked out, a thick historical fiction novel with dog-eared pages and a musty scent, so that my high and mighty parents would have to deal with the late fees, I resisted the urge. I'd already turned in my textbooks this morning before school started, but I was going to turn in my homework just because. For good or ill, I had a feeling I wasn't coming back here anytime soon.

Ash marched up to me and I frowned in perplexity. He ignored my full hands, knocked my uninjured my arm out of the way, and threw his arms around me in a hockey-player-sized bear hug. The rest of the team, who had apparently snuck in the open door behind me while I was distracted (none of them had homeroom with me), joined in on the standing-dog-pile. I grunted and managed to gasp out, "I can't breathe!"

They peeled themselves away, clapping me on the back and generally making as much noise as they were capable of, which was a lot. I hissed furiously, fully expecting the teacher to look up and give me an hour-long detention after school, but he didn't even glance up from his puzzle, faded corduroy-patched knees propped up on the corner of his desk.

A few of the other boys pushed Ash to the front of the queue, staring at the floor, suddenly nervous. He reached into the pocket of his bright blue windbreaker and pulled out a small, black felt box. He stared at the tiles and offered it shyly.

"We wanted to give you something nice to show how much we'll miss you," he explained, scuffing the toe of his sneaker on the colored tiles.

I took the box from his palm and pulled it open, the lid giving way with a soft click as the spring flexed. Inside, an oval, silver pendant rested on a silky blue cushion. The front bore my initials: *AC*; the back read *Protect her* in black cursive lettering. It was strung on a thin-linked silver chain; the links were shaped like mint leaves.

I put my hand over my heart, strangely touched. "Thank you so much, you guys." I twined my fingers through the chain, lifting it daintily from its niche. "Would you?" Andy, a big bear of a boy with a vertical cowlick and a cracked front tooth, stepped up; his thick fingers fumbled with the tiny clasp. I waited patiently, back turned, my braid flipped off to the side. He finally managed to unhook the clasp, but he had an easier time closing it around my neck. The pendant fell on my chest, standing out against the sky blue t-shirt I was wearing, just above the thorny vine applique.

Various rumors about how Andy had cracked his tooth circulated at least once a year; only those of us who had been on the hockey team with him for years knew the truth. It was, in fact, from brawling. I ought to know; that was the first, but not last, fight I had been in. It was a humdinger of a round, with everyone involved going home with at least one injury. As for me, I'd leapt into the thick of things to watch the others' backs, so my skin was mottled purple-green with bruises for weeks; I'd also broken three fingers and gained a cut on the back of the head when someone dropped a cocktail glass on me.

I threw myself into another group hug. This one wasn't as rowdy as the first, probably because I'd instigated it and not been ambushed. We held each other silently, forever the odd ones out in a preppy school that prized academics above us. Even though we had a few other sports, the lacrosse team was the one that got everything they wanted. New equipment: done. Scholarships: done. A nice bus to take them to games: done and done. The hockey team, the rowing team, and the few others we had were put on the back burner. I'm sorry, did that sound bitter?

Since I didn't feel like staying after school to return my library book, I chicken-scratched a few answers onto my incomprehensible calculus worksheet and slipped it into the 'completed work' tray, before asking for permission to head to the library. The teacher waved his hand dismissively, never once looking up from his fascinating crossword. He was deep in concentration; his thick tongue protruded from one side of his mouth like an escaping slug.

Before I left, I decided to take pity on him. I was quite good at crosswords. And logic puzzles, Sudoku, and most other puzzles, at the risk of sounding like a braggart. "Sir?"

Irritated, he glanced up, flapping the newspaper loudly on his raised knee in warning. What was he gonna do, hit me with it? "Yes?" he inquired ominously.

"I was just wondering if you needed help with your puzzle; you seem stumped. If you gave me the hint, I might be able to help."

He glared at me over his half-moon spectacles, his bushy white eyebrows popping out like twin caterpillars. He clearly hadn't expected any such gesture from me. I made my expression as innocent as possible. It was such an uncommon look for me, I'm surprised he didn't see through it right then and there.

"'A ten letter word for 'an auditory and olfactory occasion of displeasure'," he read off. I pondered it and nearly giggled when it came to me. Uh-oh. Never a good sign. I'm not a "giggler."

"Flatulence," I grinned, waving as I headed for the door, my book tucked jauntily under my arm.

It was quite a long walk to the library, but I was in no hurry. I had to walk across the school just to reach the glass double-doors. I pulled them open and stepped in, inhaling the musty scent of books. Our librarian glanced up from her book, but waved gently at me and returned to her words when she saw it was me. Maybe I wasn't a model student in other aspects, but I was the poster child for reading a lot. When we returned our books to the library, we dropped them into a thin slot; the librarian or the multiple student aides that assisted her checked it at least once a day. I dropped my book in, listening to it thud onto the pile of other books, magazines, and movies.

Since the teacher hadn't told me I needed to come back right away, I grabbed a random book from the spaced out line of "new arrivals" that ran the length of the top shelf and curled up in the corner to read. Our library had various "reading corners", little nooks with bean bags and rocking chairs to curl up and read in. I knew I didn't have to worry about getting in trouble even if I did lose track of time; the librarian, Ms. Bins, was famous for defending truants. If you wanted to get out of class and get away with it, come to the library. As long as you were reading, she didn't mind. If you weren't reading, she'd be the first to turn you in to the faculty, who occasionally called the cops.

Ms. Bins padded silently into my corner to check on me. She wore a sedate gray pencil skirt and fitted purple blouse, one of the most colorful outfits I'd ever seen her wear. Her rectangular glasses perched atop her head like some exotic bird; she'd probably forgotten they were up there again. She touched my shoulder lightly with two fingers and pressed a sticky note onto the corner of the page of my book, egregiously violating the school's "no note passing" policy. I should have known she was a rebel, with her gray flats and severe brown bun.

I heard that you're moving away. I'll miss you.

I blinked, strangely touched. That was the last thing I'd expected from her. Maybe a recommendation for a new book, but not that. I dug a stubby pencil out of the side pocket of my bag and scratched out a response beneath her neat strokes in my cramped, spidery handwriting. *Where did you hear that?*

She tilted her head cagily, like some sort of tiny bird. *Things come up in the teacher's lounge.*

I arched a brow but didn't dare ask any questions. I had a feeling they would only lead to more quandaries. *I'll miss you too*, I scratched back.

When my parents finally loaded me into the black sedan that was going to transport me to my new "school", the only thing that got me in, and kept me in, were quiet threats from my mother. *Fine*, I fumed. I'd go, but heaven help them. Hell hath no fury like an angry teenage girl. I'd be home within the week.

It took an eternity to arrive; or at least that's what it felt like. If I'd known our destination, I could've looked it up on my crappy, ancient flip phone and known exactly how long to complain about, like it took ten hours and eleven minutes to get here, that's ridiculous.

I didn't, so I had to content myself with the most obnoxious silence I'd ever heard as I watched the gray streets, and then brown trees and emerald grass, flash by through the tinted windows. I sat in the backseat with my nose in a book, a dog-eared paperback I'd dug out of my "book trunk", an expensive wooden chest meant to hold important items. I considered books important. However, my mother didn't. Uneven stacks of novels teetered dangerously beneath the lined mahogany lid. Some of them I hadn't read in months or even years, but I refused to give them away with the basic premise that I wanted them to be there if I ever did decide to read them again.

Every so often, I'd sigh or mutter under my breath. Granted, I typically mumbled things like *where'd my bookmark go?* Or *that's an ugly tree*, but the surly agents didn't need to know that. If they'd been polite to me, I might have been inclined to curb my displeasure and not take it out on them. Since they treated me like some criminal hooligan, I had no qualms about being rude; at least, no more than I usually did.

The driver was a balding, potbellied older man built like a barrel. His belly bulged against his pinstriped suit, making me suspect he hadn't been on active duty for a while. His companion was a freckled, obnoxiously red headed young man with a cracked front tooth, like Andy's, though I wasn't sure he'd gotten his from brawling. He limped on his right side; I'd heard the older man mention he'd lost a toe. It didn't affect his driving, though, when the two of them switched off to give the chubby man a chance to rest and stretch his legs. I stared moodily out the window while they traded places in the parking lot of a visitor's center. Another black sedan, exactly the same make and model as the one I was sitting in, drove slowly to the parking lot, then drove to the other side with a squeal of tires. The vehicle whipped around and parked with the shiny chrome grill facing us. I couldn't shake a bad feeling that I'd seen it before. My two nursemaids argued over the best route to take from here, fingers jabbing the map to punctuate each statement. I crawled out of the car as quietly as I could; so engrossed in their spirited conversation, the two didn't even glance back as the door clicked open and I slid across the leather seat to slip out.

The heated black of the asphalt warmed the soles of my sneakers, a welcome change from the air conditioning Antarctica that was the inside of the vehicle, the AC cranked to full blast for the past however many hours. I strode over to the other sedan, doing my best to seem nonchalant. Whoever was driving saw right through my pitiful act. The lights flared brightly and I blinked as they shone in my face, bringing flashing yellow dots to my vision even when my eyes were closed; tires and brakes squealed as the vehicle lurched once, then flew out of the parking lot. As it flashed by me, I caught a bit of the license plate and something else: a flash of dark hair and palest blue. I thumped my fist angrily on my upper thigh as I walked back to the car. I had privately thought that Chase and his merry band of nurse maids had been the ones to follow me home all those days ago, but the same combination of colors and the same make and model of the vehicle suggested differently. I could accept Chase following me, maybe, although it was a little creepy, but if it was someone else? I wasn't sure if I could deal with that.

The two stooges hadn't even noticed my absence. I settled back into my seat with a soft chuckle as I observed the pair of them. I was actually a little miffed. Whoever the higher ups of this "private school" I was being sent to, they go to the trouble of sending an attractive, persuasive man like Chase to convince my parents, set Meisha up in all of my classes and insist I be his guide, and now I got the dregs. These two couldn't stop me if I decided to run, but dang it, now I was curious. The long drive made me wonder where we I was being taken.

The frequent rest stops for my restless companions had slowed, so I figured I'd know soon enough. I was right.

Chapter Five

W hen we finally arrived, I shocked myself by liking it instantly. The place oozed sophistication and elegance, seriousness and secrets. It felt like it belonged in some kind of action-adventure novel, maybe one about spies or some kind of secret government project. My kind of place.

Wide, wrought iron gates twisted between concrete walls. Guards that rattled with weapons paced behind the closed gates. I noticed Tasers, nightsticks, pepper spray, and two different types of guns; I couldn't have told you the difference between them.

Every building in sight was hulking stone, with aluminum roofs bolted securely into place. My driver flashed an official-looking badge at a mounted camera; a mechanical voice interwoven with static feedback granted us permission to enter. The enormous gates swung open on oiled hinges, wide enough to admit us. Surly-looking guards swept the vehicle with both a machine and a canine, a leggy, energetic German Shepherd, before they allowed us to pass the guard post just inside the gates.

We rolled up in front of a large, stately building with a huge oak door that could have withstood a battering ram, the first wood in sight. Tall, sleek teenagers in t-shirts and faded jeans flowed in and out of the door almost without pause, deep in conversation with one another or hurrying to another destination with purposeful strides. They marched past us without so much as glancing in our direction, which I took to mean that they were either well-trained or simply uninterested.

The driver, whom I'd "accidentally" spilled water on at our last rest stop, opened my door for me, swinging it wide so I didn't whack my sling on it. It really had been an accident, not that he would believe that. He gestured insolently at the building, like I hadn't already figured out where we were going, thank you very much. I swung my feet out hard, inches from clipping him, and jumped out of the sedan. I wobbled slightly when I landed; my balance was screwed up with one arm in a restrictive sling.

I shoved the door open with all my one-armed might. It must have been at least a foot thick, with iron struts racing down it like slithering snakes. It was seriously heavy. I slithered through as its weight forced it shut; even then it clipped my heels, and I jolted forward a step.

Ahead of me was a long, dimly lit hallway. On the left side, it opened into a large recreation area where more slender teenagers played video games, watched TV, read a book, or napped on the mismatched furniture shoved haphazardly around, mouths open and heads tilted back. There was an air hockey table, as well as billiards. A few old fashioned arcade games were shoved in the corners. On the right, a wide doorway gave admittance to the largest kitchen I'd ever seen. Industrial refrigerators shared the room with huge cupboards, all of it ceding the floor to a magnificent marble topped island. Creamy, battered tile withstood kids standing on it, rolling ladders placed to reach unattainable food in the highest cupboards, and bar stools squeaking into place at the island. Teens ate, happy smiles and chatter around the room, playful shoving and stealing of food present.

My stomach rumbled like a whale call, which I interpreted as my cue to leave before anyone glanced up to see what it was. I strode down the carpeted hallway, dodging people popping out of the various rooms. With no instructions, I guessed I was meant to enter the room at the end of the hall, an office of some sort, door closed. A long-limbed, attractive brunette boy patiently waited his turn. He dipped a courteous nod to me, leaning against the hard wall.

The door opened, revealing a slim teenage girl; she blew past me without acknowledging my existence, which I thought was a little rude. The boy threw me an exasperated look and stepped into the office, pulling the door closed behind him.

The conversation of the boy ahead of me took only a few minutes. I couldn't hear what was said, but the smile on his face told me the outcome. He waved as he walked by, revealing an older man standing in the doorway.

"Please, come in," he encouraged politely. He'd already turned, hobbling stiffly back to his desk. Mounds of paper struggled for attention, sticking out at odd angles and looking like a paper tempest waiting to happen. He sank into his high-backed leather chair in relief; I took my cue to plop down in the chair on my side, directly across from him. A sheet of paper fluttered off the stack; I lunged to snatch it, placing it carefully on top of the pile it had come from.

"You have good reflexes," the man noted. I waited; that didn't seem to require an answer.

"My name is Hale. I am the director of a private program called Rediscovery," he began. "Do you believe in dragons?"

I blinked and hesitated. What an odd question to start a conversation with. "I want to," I hazarded cautiously. This line of questioning seemed like a trap. He looked impressed at my response; his bushy white eyebrows fluttered up and then down.

"Good. Because you've found them."

"Explain," I demanded. Where was he going with this?

"Twenty years ago, an ambitious group of researchers went back to an old idea, one that others had long ago given up on: If they could find genetic material from an extinct creature, they could resurrect it. They could create an infant, something that could be studied in each stage of development, could be raised and trained for their purposes. They would gain recognition from their peers. Needless to say, finding a large sample from an extinct creature is quite difficult," he added wryly; I nodded.

"In 2018, after years of fruitless work, they decided to search near an area where they'd already looked. None of them really expected to find anything; they were just going through the motions. So imagine their surprise when they found a large, hard stone the likes of which they'd never seen. A meteor, perhaps? Definitely something that they could use to redeem themselves." His eyes looked dreamy and unfocused, no longer here with me in his disorganized office.

"And?" I prompted gently. I hated to break him out of his reverie, but I was curious. This story was fascinating, but I wanted him to get to the good part. He shook himself.

"They searched that area for weeks in the hopes of finding something else. During that time, the 'meteor' hatched. The young dragon within bonded with a young research assistant. A dozen more had been found, which meant they had to do nothing, only wait for them to hatch." He rubbed a hand roughly over his face, voice abruptly grim. "An adult dragon, most likely an accidental hatching, attacked and killed a scientist. We-they ran for their lives with the eggs they'd worked so hard to find. Few of the eggs hatched. In fact, there is one that has been waiting all this time," he finished. I was so engrossed I almost missed his slip. Almost. Had he been part of that expedition?

"So you have dragons," I nodded. My heart was pounding in my chest, and I could hardly contain myself. "I can believe that, once you show me some proof. Lots of proof, soon."

Hale chuckled indulgently. "I understand. I would want proof too, if I was in your shoes." He stood slowly, grasping the wooden cane that I hadn't noticed leaning against his desk, hobbling slowly to the door, which he opened. He poked his head out and spoke, but I couldn't hear what he was saying. A minute later, the brunette boy from earlier returned, a leather messenger bag with an odd bulge slung over his shoulder. He cradled it to his chest like it contained the thing that was most precious to him in the world. I opened my mouth to ask what was going on, but before I could, the flap moved. As I stared in fascination, a tiny face poked from under the flap, forked pink tongue flicking. The little animal was jade green, it's mouth filled with teeth that looked deceptively sharp for how small they were. I shifted and the tiny thing retreated with a startled squeal. Hale thanked the boy and sent him on his way; with another shy wave, he left. I stared after him.

"So that's proof," I acknowledged breathily. "But what am I doing here?"

"We want you to be the public face of all dragons. The figurehead, if you will. As such, you will be schooled in the matter of all things dragon," he explained.

"Real-life skills you won't find anywhere else," I recalled, thinking back to what oily Chase had told my parents as one of the selling points. Hale nodded and smiled; he obviously had a basic idea of what Chase had said. Maybe it was a selling pitch. "So I'll get my own dragon?"

"Yes," Hale agreed. "As well as training, but I'm sure you'd like to explore before you make any decisions." He pressed a button on his desk. Chase popped his head in, long dust blond locks wet and tousled. "Alex will need a guide. Would you?"

"Sure," Chase agreed. "Just give me a minute."

I popped out of my chair, but calmed myself when I realized I probably looked like a jack in the box. Chase gestured rudely at me to follow him. His hair was still soaked, drenching the shoulders of his gray t-shirt. He walked ahead of me, just barely in earshot, weaving easily through the crowds of people who called out to us. Or rather, him.

I hate to admit it, but I didn't need to explore to know what my decision was. I felt some tug that begged me to stay, this place I had hated in words but loved in everything else. I didn't know whether it was the destination, the beautiful buildings, the teens who seemed so like me in only passing observation, or the promise of dragons.

I'd been obsessed with dragons as a child, and my no-nonsense mother had broken my heart when she informed me mercilessly that they weren't real. I hadn't wanted to believe her, but everything pointed to their nonexistence. In all the stories I'd read as a child, about dragons being the villain, I just couldn't see it that way. At first, my mom had tried to convince me that dragons were bad, that I shouldn't have figurines and memorabilia of them all over my room. Eventually she had given up on that, and pounded that dragons were make-believe into my head. She had taken away anything related to dragons and hidden it, but I had still secretly rooted for the dragons and sought out anything related to them. I had boxes full of stuff shoved into my closet, away from my mother's prying eyes.

Dragons were real again, to someone other than me, and I was determined to be a part of it. Dragons were real, and suddenly giving up my family, friends, and everything I'd ever known would be a small price to pay if I could show the world, especially my mother, once and for all that they were real. I was determined to see this through. I'd left everything behind, but I could make this my home. And I would.

Chapter Six

News flash: Chase hates me. Oh, he gave me the tour alright, but he spoke in such a monotone it took all my self-control not to burst out laughing, and when I did finally lose it, he glared at me like I'd poked him with a pin. Whatever. Next time I was requesting a new guide. Maybe Meisha, who'd waved enthusiastically every time I'd seen him.

Chase pointed out the pertinent points: the barracks, six long, low bunkers, the training arena, farthest away from the house, and the loft. The loft was not at all what you'd expect from its moniker; the dragons slept there. Inside, it was the most erratic thing I have ever seen, but it had a sort of chaotic, unorganized beauty that lessened its overwhelming-ness. Steel perches jutted unpredictably from the walls; dragons and riders lazed on them, not seeming to notice the huge drop to the hard floor below. The highest perches could only be reached on dragonback, which meant the older dragons had no competition for them. The ones near floor level had squat ladders connecting them to the ground.

A tiny yellow hatchling played with a rider on the lowest level. It was an ugly mustard yellow color, but it didn't matter. I stared and swallowed hard, searching for a way to reconcile what I was seeing with what I had been told all my life. Despite the little one that I had seen earlier, and what I was seeing now, it was a bit of a shock. The little dragon took an overzealous swipe with its right front paw and tumbled in slow motion toward the concrete. I gasped, covering my mouth in horror. He squealed, flaring his tiny wings and flopping ungracefully to the ground, unharmed. His rider hurried down the ladder and dropped from a few rungs up, scooping him up and crooning gently to him, cuddling against his chest and rocking him.

"I'm Syren," the man introduced, juggling the tiny beast into the crook of one arm and extending his hand to shake. He was in his early twenties, tall and broad-shouldered, with close-cropped sandy blonde hair. The dragon wriggled free of his grip and crawled around his neck. Syren leaned forward so he didn't fall off the back, not seeming to mind being hunched like Quasimodo.

"Alex Chevalier. Is he yours?" I cringed, belatedly realizing that what just came out of my mouth was astronomically rude. Syren took it all in stride.

"No," he answered good-naturedly.

"Syren is the hatchling trainer," Chase explained. "He helps train hatchlings and riders in the first stages of development as a pair."

"This little guy," Syren said, knuckling the dragon gently on the top of his head, producing a high-pitched squeal of delight, "has a rider in the sick bay. I'm watching out for him." He made a wry face as the hatchling licked his throat. "Not that I'm doing a great job at the moment."

I nodded, but Syren was already gone, striding over to chastise a rider for some wrong I hadn't seen. I drank in the dragons. I couldn't believe how beautiful they were. Every color you could think of, from the basic rainbow, to the gleaming shine of polished gemstones. Some had other markings: splotches like paint horses, spots like cheetahs or leopards. One, a holly green dragon, even had stripes, bright red against his neck and extending to his throat. Some of them had paler markings on their bellies or marks like spectacles that ringed their eyes; none looked even remotely the same.

"You'll meet the others later. Right now, we need to find you an egg," Chase said curtly. I followed him out reluctantly, throwing one last longing look over my shoulder.

"Welcome to the hatchery," Chase announced. He'd hauled a heavy sliding door aside, sand spilling over the raised edge. As soon as I was in, he pulled it shut; it nearly closed on the heels of my ratty tennis shoes. I glared. What was the hurry?

"It's better for the eggs," he said softly, the first sign of contrition I had seen from him so far. The room was smoking hot, literally. Small fires blazed in sunken pits at intervals. Grainy sand heaped unevenly around the room, littered with shards of some pliable material that flexed and bent between my fingers when I picked it up.

"Eggshell. Find your egg." I honestly had no idea what would happen from here on out. Would I stay here even after I "graduated"? What kind of dragon would choose me? I took a deep breath and stepped forward. Whatever happened, happened.

"How?" I asked, frowning.

"You'll know," he said simply. *Oh, gee. Thanks. Real helpful.* I rolled my eyes, walking aimlessly around the pits. Eggs of every color rested in their cradles, so still and silent it was hard to believe they held something alive.

Transparent white, eggplant purple, turquoise blue, jade green. They flashed by. My heart sank with each step. I was beginning to wonder if they'd made a mistake. If I couldn't bond with an egg, then what?

My feet swerved, taking me without my consent toward a pit in the darkest corner. The black egg was covered in a thin patina of dust, the flame beneath it orange and guttering, like no one had bothered to tend it. It hung from thin crisscrossed chains, forming a sort of basket over the fire. I swiped it off reflexively, sweeping away the dust with my palm. The surface was warm, like sliding into a bathtub that was not too hot, not too cold.

A pair of gloves appeared in my peripheral vision; I flinched. They were made of old, thick leather, blackened with soot at the fingertips. They were elbow-length, like falconers gloves. I took them, unsure of what I was supposed to do.

"Take it out," Chase ordered. My eyes flashed up to his face. *Was he nuts?* There was no possible way I was sticking my hands into a fire. Even as weak and guttering as this one was, I was pretty sure it could still burn me. He made an encouraging gesture, so obviously he wasn't kidding, like I'd thought he was. His arm muscles tightened as he crossed his arms over his broad chest.

I swiped my sweaty palms on my jeans and slid them into the wide wrist holes of the gloves. The tough leather scraped, making me want to itch. Before I could think it through, I plunged my hands into the fire, grasped the egg, and yanked it out.

For a scary second, my gloves scrabbled for purchase on the slick surface; I was terrified it would fly out of my hands and become Humpty- Dumpty. I dug my fingers into it, placing it gently on the sandy floor in front of my kneecaps.

"Put it in your lap," Chase advised. "It needs the warmth."

I crossed my legs crisscross applesauce and picked it up carefully. A spidery crack appeared, pearl white against the luminescent black of the egg. I nearly fumbled it out of my hands in shock, followed by grim humor. If I dropped it, there'd definitely be cracks in it.

It rocked from side to side, like a dysfunctional spinning top. I was fascinated, but for some reason, so was Chase.

"I would have thought you'd seen plenty of eggs hatch," I observed mulishly, my eyes glued to the egg.

"I have," he remarked offhandedly. "But this egg has been waiting twenty years. None of us knew if it would ever hatch. We were worried it was damaged or defective." I felt a strange surge or protectiveness for whatever was in the egg. I knew what it was like to be different, though, to my knowledge at least, no one had ever called me "defective."

The egg crumbled slowly, pieces of shell sloughing off the sides like shale from a mountain face. I jerked back like I'd been stung when an angular head popped up, a piece of egg perched on its crown. The remainder of the egg fell away. The creature shook like a dog, from head to tail. The dragon snuffled, crawling out of my legs and putting its nose to the ground, like a bloodhound. Its tail swished back and forth and one of the dusky gray spikes buried itself in my palm.

I yelped and the dragon squealed. It reared up on its short hind legs and flared its wings, struggling to remove the spike embedded in my palm. I soothed it reflexively, crooning gently while I wiggled the spike out. It dropped to all fours, tilting its head and mewling, acid green eyes upturned. I held out my hand; it had been tucked against my side, but it was obvious the dragon wanted to check on it. Its forked tongue swiped the wound. I couldn't figure out whether it tickled or hurt.

"Ow," I said, just in case. My hand was still bleeding sluggishly; the dragon wouldn't leave it be. "Is it going to get infected now?" I asked resignedly.

Chase tilted his head as he considered. "No," he decided. "Dragon saliva is excellent at cleaning wounds. If they clean it, it almost never becomes infected."

"Dragons have magic spit?" I checked, just to make sure I'd heard correctly. He grinned lopsidedly.

"Close enough," he agreed. "Come on. We'll have dinner at the house and then you and your new friend can get some rest."

Chapter Seven

"That was so good!" I said enthusiastically. For some reason, even though I'd only eaten a few hours ago, I'd been starving. I'd shoveled food onto my plate, barely noticing the knowing glances passed between the riders. A few of the hatchlings, including my little black beast, had chased each other around; they'd occasionally stolen food, leaping up like a flying fish to grab something and disappear. Mine especially seemed to prefer the thick sausage links, which was odd, since I did too.

A thought suddenly occurred to me; the dragon riders around the table were definitely the best ones to ask. "Wait. How do I name my dragon? How will I know?"

Syren shook his head and grinned. "You don't name them. She'll let you know."

I only got one part of the whole exchange. "Rewind," I said, twirling my index finger in the air and making a time-out T with my hands. It was a little awkward with one arm in a sling, but I managed. "She will let me know. How do you know it's a she?"

Syren looked surprised; he glared at Chase, who looked sheepish. "You didn't tell her?" he reproached, earning a shrug from Chase, who was tomato-red.

Syren turned to me. "Female dragons grow to be larger and have ridges on the underside of their tails."

He reached for her, giving me a look as if to ask permission, which I suppose was only polite. I nodded my consent. He flipped the little dragon deftly to her back, wrapping her tail around his hand. Tiny bumps ranged from her hindquarters to the tip.

She wriggled, making it clear she wanted to be put down. He let her go and she padded across the wooden dinner table to me, which probably wasn't sanitary. Her tail swept a piece of abandoned broccoli off a rider's plate; he grabbed it with a long-suffering look and popped it in his mouth.

I'd finished my meal, and my dragon was curled contentedly around my throat, like a black feather boa. I could see her tiny muzzle on one side of my face, strong and smooth, acid green eyes closed. She had ridges above her eyebrows and her scales continued down onto her eyelid, which I hadn't expected. The scales on her eyelid were foggy gray; it made it appear that she was wearing smoky eyeshadow. She naturally had more makeup than me, which wasn't hard, since I didn't wear makeup. Lucky girl.

I considered the table. The other riders all sat back, hands folded across flat stomachs, with contented looks on their faces. Something else I noticed as I was studying them: they had strange eyes. The boys had black rings at the outer edge of their irises; the girls had similar gold rings. Some had bigger rings, some smaller, but they all had them. One girl, with smoky red hair and creamy, translucent skin, had such a large gold ring that it split the iris perfectly with the natural blue. It was a strange look, and I couldn't stop staring.

"Where do those come from?" I asked, gesturing to my own eye, in reference to their own. They looked confused.

"What are you talking about?" one asked in confusion.

"Never mind," I said quickly. If they didn't know right off what I was talking about, I wasn't going to pursue it. I yawned hugely; my dragon mimicked, her forked pink tongue flicking out between her lips like a snake's. I turned my head while she was still yawning and got the full view of her tonsils. The skin of her throat seemed almost like it had scales as well, and had a shiny, almost metallic sheen to it, like fireproof clothing. I wondered offhandedly if that was to protect her throat when she breathed fire, but my fluttering eyelids convinced me it could wait until later.

"Tired?" Syren asked understandingly.

"Yeah," I admitted sheepishly. I had been trying to wait out the others, and refused to admit that I was tired, but it was a losing battle. If I didn't go soon, I'd end up face first on my plate. My dragon had licked it clean, so it wasn't dirty, but there you go.

"Would someone take her back to the hatchery?" he asked.

"Why?" I asked curiously. Not that I didn't want to sleep, because I very much did, but Chase had shown me the barracks. Why wasn't I sleeping there?

"New dragons and riders stay in the hatchery for the first few days, to get to know each other before you start your training," he explained.

"Oh," I nodded.

"I'll take you," a familiar voice volunteered. I whipped my head toward the opposite end of the table. Meisha leaned forward with a grin, waving shyly and nodding approvingly at my little black, who sat upright on my shoulder with an interested titter, the bumps on the underside of her tail scraping my throat where it was wrapped around my neck. I tugged gently and she loosened it reluctantly, tightening it again and flapping her wings for balance when I rose from my seat. I waved to the other riders and said my goodbyes, careful not to step on any of the other- what were they called? Hatchlings? - on the way out the door. The bright glow of the riders' grins followed me out.

I followed him back to the hatchery in the gloaming. The sun was just setting, cradled in a nest of violet, sky blue and tangerine. He led me around the side of the hatchery and to a back door, pulling it open and standing back to allow me to enter first. Ever the gentleman.

The back of the hatchery was vastly different from the front. Small rooms branched off haphazardly, like a tree, with branches extending out in all directions. The doors had no writing to identify them, but a few did have long, jagged gouges, which I guessed were claw marks. Temper tantrum, or something more sinister?

Kidding. I imagined young dragons were just as bad as their human counterparts.

Meisha consulted a clipboard hanging from a small peg on the wall and grabbed the ballpoint pen strung with it, scrawling something in the chart on the middle of the page.

"What room you're in," he explained, waving me through one of the few doors with no claw marks. "You'll be staying here for the next few days, except for meals and such. After that, you guys will start your training. If there's anything you need, just ask. Good night," he added hurriedly, backing away and waving.

"Good night," I called at his retreating back. I stepped inside, cradling my dragon, who was loose with exhaustion. She flopped over my good arm like one of those towels a butler carried in old-fashioned movies.

I surveyed the room. A short cot was shoved into one corner, an ancient steamer trunk was in another, and a small nightstand held a pitcher of water, a short glass, and a small leather-bound book, like a journal. The glass was shining clean; I wondered distractedly how often this room was used. The pitcher was stoppered, I assumed to keep dust out and such.

I pulled open the steamer trunk, loosening the thick, studded leather straps. My dragon was flopped on the bed, moaning piteously. She lay on her back, swishing her tail over the edge and staring at me upside down. It made me dizzy just looking at her.

"You're fine." I laughed. "Give me a few minutes." She snorted grumpily and curled up on my pillow, staking her claim. She'd probably be extremely hard to move later, but I supposed that was what I got for making her wait.

The trunk had interesting contents. Old fashioned mason jars full of meat cluttered the bottom. A velvety purple cushion rested upright against the side; a pair of black fingerless gloves flipped carelessly over the lip of a short metal bucket. There were mismatched stacks of clothing, in various sizes and colors; one thing they all had in common were the strange leather patches on the shoulders and wrists. Several brushes and rags were tossed into a small tin bucket, a clear vial of something nestled in the rags. What looked to be some sort of nail file or hasp was jammed in there as well.

An off-white, slightly crumpled paper explained the function of the items. The cushion was for the dragon to sleep on; I thought it was safe to disregard that for now, seeing as my dragon was flopped lazily on my bed, waiting for me to come, having given up on her piteous cries. The mason jars contained meats that I would learn to mix my dragon's favorite food with. I could get the meat in bulk once I figured it out. There was a jar of strips containing bacon, beef, chicken, lobster, pork, and turkey. The bucket was to mix the strips, deep enough to hold everything but not so big that she couldn't reach her food. The gloves were for me. The other bucket, the one stuffed with seemingly innocuous items, was for cleaning the little creature. The nail file was to keep her claws sharp, with the cloths to wash her off and the vial to keep her wings healthy and strong, as well as to alleviate itching. Itching from what?

The page explained that eventually my dragon's scales would become sharp at certain angles; the fingerless gloves would protect me from getting cut. They were thin and faded, the black thread peeling away in some places and patched in others. I pulled them on, wiggling my fingers for a few moments, then tugged them off and replaced them in the trunk.

I had a throbbing ache behind my right eye, so I gave up on my explorations and stretched out on the cot, curling carefully around my dragon so I didn't disturb her. I stroked one of the cloths lightly across her ebony scales, feeling their hardness tickle my fingertips through the thin cloth as I swiped away infinitesimal motes of dust. She huffed softly, and peeled one eye open.

Something popped into my head: *S*. I lifted my head, puzzled, the cloth stopping mid-motion. That was out of the blue; I didn't recall thinking about that before it popped into my mind. Another letter popped up: *T*. My dragon's eyes were open now; she had what could only be described as a sarcastic 'duh' expression. An idea formed in my head, but I wasn't at all sure if I was right.

"Is that you?" I asked suspiciously. She huffed, which I took as a yes. Then I recalled what Syren had said: *You don't name them. She'll let you know*. "Is that it?" I asked. "You want me to guess?" Another huff; I racked my brain.

"Star? Stacy? Stefanie? Stella?" I guessed. She kept that weird look on her face, which I understood to be no, up until the final name. "Am I close?"

She jerked her chin up, nearly a nod. For some reason, all I could think about was a hockey scout's reviews of me: stellar form, superb grace, he'd said. "Stellar!" I said suddenly, and was rewarded with a gentle chirp, low in her throat. "Alright, Stellar," I yawned. "Time to get some sleep." She chirped again, tucking against my rib cage and draping her tail possessively over my wrist. She was asleep before I was, but not by much.

Dark. My eyes shot open. "What?"

Dark, she repeated.

"You mean night," I realized suddenly. She must have heard the others calling out "good night" and proffered her own version, the best she could with limited understanding. "Dark," I agreed, patting her tenderly and stretching back out once I slid my sling over my head. She curled up on my stomach, and I fell asleep to her contented purr.

Chapter Eight

S *cree!* I shot to awareness, reaching instinctively for Stellar, who wasn't at my side. She was in the doorway, frolicking around a dark-haired boy, who waited patiently to be invited in.

"Are you a vampire?" I joked sleepily, rubbing my eyes blearily to scrub the sleep-crust out of them. "Need to be invited in?"

He laughed gently. "No. Just trying to be polite. I'm Orion, by the way."

After I had waved him in, and he approached, I could see why he was called that. A pattern of freckles on his right cheekbone mapped out a miniature version of the constellation Orion on his tanned skin. It was the weirdest, and coolest, birthmark I'd ever seen.

He strode over to the steamer trunk, loosening the straps and pulling out the mason jars one by one. I swung my legs over the side of the cot, my legs jolting when they encountered the cold floor. He sat them down in alphabetical order, from left to right, more organized than I could ever be. He pulled a strip out of each, slicing off a chunk and dropping them in a small plastic bowl. He passed the bowl to me, and I extended it to Stellar, making a mental note of which meats she seemed to prefer. Bacon, beef, chicken, and pork.

"One at a time," Orion advised; I pulled the strips out of the jar one at a time and tossed them into the bucket.

Stellar, who had wandered out into the hallway to explore, surged through the doorway and plunged headfirst into the bucket. Her wings flapped and her tail thumped against the sides. She gobbled the strips down in huge, gulping bites, bobbing her head like a stork trying to swallow a fish. Orion and I took one look at one another and burst out laughing.

I studied him from the corner of my eye as Stellar gulped her meal. His raven-black hair was of medium length, the straight strands just brushing his collarbone and curving against the back of his neck. The bright blue eyes, set above his strange birthmark, were determined and focused, with the same black ring around the irises I'd noted in the other riders.

A long pink tongue flashed past us and gathered up a stray strip of meat from the floor. Orion reached back without looking, stroking the dragon's head and throat, producing a low hum of pleasure. This dragon was fully grown, and probably taller at the shoulder than I was. He was deep blue on his back, with wings the color of the Caribbean ocean, the dark blue lightening to periwinkle and turquoise on his nose, muzzle, and belly. His elegant head reminded me of a thoroughbred, with the same liquid, expressive eyes.

Stellar had curled up on her cushion, laid out on my cot next to my pillow. I could hear her low purr. Even curled up in a tightly coiled ball as she was, I could have sworn that she had grown overnight. From what I had heard from the other riders, hatchlings did grow abnormally quickly, so it was possible. I had been warned to remember that she was young, even when she grew to be my height or taller. If I didn't, it would be easy to overlook the things she didn't know, or simply hadn't had the chance to learn yet. Upon further exploration of the room, I had found a leather bound book filled with pictures of anything I could think of and more, along with other teaching aids that would help me to teach Stellar. Each night before bed, I had flipped through the photo album and showed her the pictures, doing my best to teach her what they meant. It was like teaching a preschooler. She was a quick learner, but I couldn't help but think that she would have learned quicker if she had a better teacher.

"We should let her sleep," Orion told me quietly. "You have other things to do, and Tyne can watch over her while we're gone."

I stood and stretched, my legs stiff after sitting cross-legged for so long. Tyne settled himself next to my bedside table, extending his muzzle to lay it beside Stellar's sleeping form. His large eyes followed us until we left the room.

"Where are we going?" I asked as we strode down the hallway. I had long legs, but I still had to lengthen my strides in order to keep pace with him.

"You need to be fitted for rider's clothes," he answered.

"No one was wearing any special clothing yesterday," I pointed out. All of the riders I'd seen yesterday were wearing t-shirts and jeans of various types and colors. Not one of them wore anything that would be out of place in a shopping mall or any other place where teenagers frequented.

Orion flushed sheepishly. "We didn't want to scare you away," he admitted. "And it may also have been laundry day."

I just grinned to myself and shook my head. That made sense.

Neither of us said much until we got to a door labeled "The Clothes Room." Orion pulled the thick door open, gesturing politely for me to go first. Someone inside reached past me, snatched Orion's wrist, and yanked him inside. He was so startled he flailed, grabbed my wrist, and ended up yanking me in after him. We nearly tumbled into a pile, but I stopped myself just in time.

A woman, whose head wouldn't have reached any higher than my shoulder, scolded Orion in another language. Her long, slender index finger prodded him in the chest, and he backed away until he fetched up against the wall. I shifted, not quite sure if he needed help or not. If he did, what would I do? Anything that I would normally have done would hurt her, and I was reluctant to cause harm to such a tiny woman.

She spun and saw me. The change was as sudden as someone had flipped a switch. She spoke a few words, enough for my rudimentary, high school French to recognize a greeting, before she remembered herself and switched to English.

"Hello, hello!" she bubbled, her accent thick and rich as warm butter. "You must be Alex! Oh, you are so beautiful," she said dreamily, eyes misty. Her fingers gripped my chin lightly before stepping back to study me. Her full, pale pink lips moved without a sound.

"You!" she barked suddenly. Her blue eyes blazed. Orion flinched. "I will deal with you later," she warned ominously. I pressed my lips together. His terror of such a diminutive woman was almost comical, but I had a feeling that tight peplum top was held in place by a spine of steel.

"Yes, Madame LaVarne," he mumbled, and slipped out as soon as her back was turned.

"I do so love it when I have good models to work with," she gushed. She studied a strand of my hair and my face, tapping her chin with a finger. Her slender hands pulled my arms to the sides and front, then she clicked her tongue and hurried over to a trestle table. She scooped up a measuring tape and wrapped it around my hips, making notes on Post-its.

I sat down on a short wooden stool, my knees practically to my chest, as she picked up various rolls of fabric and studied them critically, pulling the material free of its binding and holding it up to the light to view it better. Leather, velvet, satin, cotton, wool and chiffon, and many others that I couldn't name.

"Come back tomorrow," she decided finally. Her decision was to pull several materials out of the pile and dump them onto another one, so tall and unwieldy I tensed in preparation of it falling off. "And remind that boy to come back later."

I couldn't believe my ears. "It'll only take you one day to make my uniform?"

She laughed like I'd made a joke. I hadn't, but maybe she'd seen it as one.

Meisha poked his head in, motioning for me to follow him. I waved shyly at Madame LaVarne, who returned the gesture with considerably more enthusiasm and had already turned away to begin working as I exited. Meisha was waiting patiently outside. "Your training starts tomorrow," he informed me. "Someone will wake you when it's time. No doubt Madame LaVarne will have your uniform done by then. She's very discerning about that."

"What about my uniform? And Stellar?"

"Your uniform will be ready. And Syren will watch her. She'll be fine with him."

"What am I supposed to do until then?" It sounded a little like I was whining, which I hadn't meant, but boredom was not high on my list of top things. Strange things come about when I'm bored. Not necessarily bad things, but strange.

"Rest up. Trust me, you'll be glad you did," he said fervently. I should have taken his advice. Instead, I had spent the next few hours discovering the best way to care for Stellar, which was interesting to say the least. She had so much energy to expend that I could hardly keep up with her, although I did my best. I went through the routine spelled out on the paper as best I could, struggling to clean her double eyelids with a cloth as she wriggled. I hadn't noticed that there were two sets because they looked exactly the same, with the difference only being visible when she dropped the second set. Oiling her wings took the longest, and left me sweaty and panting by the end, alot like giving a dog a bath. It was a nightmare for me and a fun game of keep-away for her. I cleaned up as best I could and scooped her up to take to dinner that night, which raised both of our spirits considerably.

As I padded across the floor to my cot that night, I stepped on something sharp, barely swallowing a yelp even in my exhausted state. When I crouched down to see what it was, I came up with a tiny white tooth, a perfect match to the gap that flashed in Stellar's mouth as she yawned. I grinned and crawled into bed, and didn't wake up until morning.

Chapter Nine

Someone knocked lightly on my door. I sat up slowly, rubbing my eyes blearily with my knuckles.

"Who is it?" I mumbled.

A dark, curly head poked in. "Time to wake up, ma'am," the girl said shyly. "If you don't, you won't have time to get dressed before you speak to Hale; you have your lessons following that."

I threw off my covers, sending Stellar flying. She flapped her wings indignantly and managed to hop far enough off the thin blanket that she didn't get flung completely across the room. She sent a blood red jag into my mind and my right temple throbbed fiercely.

"Sorry," I murmured.

"You don't need to get dressed!" the girl blurted; she flushed when I arched a brow at her. "Just throw on a jacket. You'll be getting your uniform soon anyway."

I grabbed a hoodie with a pouch on the stomach. The top bore the cartoonish design of a water lily. I tucked Stellar carefully into the pocket. Her head poked out the side like a baby kangaroo. I swallowed a laugh, but she didn't bother. A colorful rainbow ghosted across my mind as I slid my necklace over my head and clasped it in the back, peeling my hair out of the way and into a rushed ponytail.

"Ready," I lied.

The girl was already off; her curly black bob rippled with each stride. I had no trouble keeping up with her. She had sun streaks in her black hair, making her look absurdly like a skunk with a dye job. Her ears were pierced from the lobe all the way up into the cartilage; I could see the hole in her nose where another stud would go.

"Where's your stud?" I asked, gesturing to my long, straight nose. My ears were pierced, but I rarely wore anything large in them. They had been ripped out on more than one occasion, but I never seemed to learn. The girl tilted her head and grinned. "When my dragon was a hatchling, she got her claw stuck in it and ripped it out. I can't smell anything anymore; I don't want that to happen again."

I winced. *Yowch. That had to hurt.* I studied this girl's uniform, wondering if they were all the same. Was my uniform going to be one-of-a-kind or an old hand-me-down from one of the old steamer trunks I'd seen in the periphery of the room yesterday?

"Alex!" Madame LaVarne murmured happily. She didn't seem to notice that it was five in the morning; to be fair, I hadn't either until I'd gone back to fetch my watch off my bedside table and seen what time it was. My eyes had gone googly.

"Hoodie off," Madame LaVarne ordered briskly. I edged Stellar out of the pocket; she chimed gently when Madame LaVarne patted her on the head, carefully keeping her long, starry-blue nails out of the way. A hangnail snagged in the hoodie as I peeled it off; I was hung up for a second until I could wriggle out of it. Stellar chimed in laughter. The side of Madame LaVarne's mouth quirked up in an amused half-smile before she hid it behind one delicate hand.

She collected a stack of material off a table and skinned something off the top. A long sleeved, body-hugging turtleneck with black leather patches on my shoulders and from my elbows to the backs of my hands. It had a thin black circle around my neck; below that it started with navy and went through shades of blue and purple, fading to a gentle lilac. Sleek black cargo pants, made with what seemed like legging-material, equipped with two deep pockets on either side, were held up with a wide black belt, studded with raised turquoise circles.

Thicker leather patches were adhered to the insides of the calves and thighs.

I slid into the clothes, surprised at how well they fit me. The top hugged my curves; the colors both drew attention to the good parts, my chest and abs, and turned attention away from the bad, the thick, ropy scar you could just barely see the outline of in the shirt. The cargo pants bunched at the top of my ankles, even with the belt. The turquoise circles coordinated perfectly with the shirt. Madame LaVarne was a genius.

"Oh!" Madame LaVarne laughed. "I almost forgot."

She bent under one of the trestle tables on the other side of the room, digging around and coming up with a pair of boots. They were calf-highs, black with a zipper up the side. I kicked off my tennis shoes, unsure whether to leave my socks on or take them off. Madame LaVarne opened the top of a boot, showing me the creamy interior; there was a tiny pocket hidden in the left side. "You put a knife here," she explained. "No one will know it's there unless you tell them. No one can see it from the outside. Also, you won't need to wear socks. When they start to smell, pull the lining out and wash it; simple."

"Thank you," I said sincerely. She'd gone to all this trouble, hurried through it, to ensure that I had a uniform that flattered me. With one day and a few minutes' worth of measurement, she had managed to create a look that suited me and made me feel even more confident than I already did. I was grateful for that.

"You're welcome," she smiled. "Hurry; your classes start soon. Drop Stellar off at the Loft with Syren before you go to the training arena."

I hurried after the girl; I noted offhand that she hadn't bothered to introduce herself.

"What's your name?" I hinted. She started.

"I didn't say?" I arched an eyebrow; my expression saying, "Would I have asked if you did?" "I'm Mia," she grumbled, tanned skin flushed sunburn-red. "Keep up or you'll make us both late. I'm not going to be punished because you're too slow."

Excuse me? That attitude was quite different from the one she'd displayed on the way over. I considered slowing my strides even more, just out of spite, but it was probably not a good idea to gain enemies so soon. In fact, I could use all the allies I could get.

Chapter Ten

The weirdest thing about my first day of training: our instructors were David and Goliath. David was the weapons instructor; a hulking bear of a man with a full beard that he kept braided and tied back. His hair was cougar tawny, nearly red, and pulled into a ponytail. His dragon was Goliath, who would be one of Stellar's instructors, when she was finally old enough to fly. Eventually, we'd fly together.

"Again!" David barked. I picked up a blunted practice knife from the table, pulled back, took aim down the blade, and flicked my wrist. The tip impaled itself an inch from the center of the target, tauntingly close for my first day. I picked up another without instruction, throwing it. It hit the yellow center straight on. Of the thirty or more practice knives I'd thrown today, my first day of training, the last was the only one to hit the target.

"Woohoo!" I cheered. My fists pumped. Other riders stopped what they were doing to give me a strange look, but I didn't care. This was the same feeling I'd had when I had just started hockey, watching those first few goals sink into the white net and drinking in the roar of the crowd. I hadn't thought that anything could beat that feeling, but I was wrong.

David was unmoved. "Again."

An hour later, I collapsed, panting and gasping. My lungs felt like they were starving for air. David had explained to me, in his booming voice, why he was pushing me so hard. I'd seen how different he was with others, in the sparse moments of rest he'd given me today, and demanded to know why he was treating me differently. Stellar and I were to become a messenger pair, to carry messages in conditions no one else could. When helicopters and planes were grounded, we'd be up. If the situation in a country wouldn't allow military personnel to deliver, we'd be up.

Messenger dragons were the best of the best. There were heavy, swift, gathering, and messenger teams, called hunts. Stellar and I were to be trained as solos, riders and dragons specifically trained to deliver messages alone, with no backup. Heavy dragons lived up to their names, mammoth, thick-legged-and-necked beasts with vast wings. Their job was to carry men and supplies to and from their destination. Swift hunts were streamlined, speedy dragons without an ounce of fat on them; they scouted ahead in areas where larger dragons would have stuck out like a sore thumb, careful not to be seen, while their riders took note of the particulars: troop movement, placement, numbers, supplies, etc. and flew back to base with all speed.

Dragons were omnivores, who could eat nearly anything. They ate primarily meat and fish, with plants supplementing it. The gathering hunts fished, hunted, and harvested edible plants in areas kept by Project Rediscovery for that specific purpose. The plants were mixed in with the meat we gave them, to provide flavor and certain health benefits. Stellar preferred mint and catnip plants in hers; don't ask me why, I don't know. Maybe she was a cat in a past life.

All dragons looked different. Chase had taken me around to meet examples of each. Mona, a swift dragon, was daintier than I'd expected from a dragon. She was the off-white of raw sugar granules, a tiny, deer like creature, with horn nubs on the top of her head. Her rider encouraged me to touch the nubs, which were velveteen soft and fuzzy. Her tail was short, like a Doberman's, and I wondered if they had docked it. The crown of her head only reached the top of my shoulder. I hoped fervently that Stellar would grow bigger than that. Her wings were what I really noticed: they were soft as felt and stretched paper thin. Goliath was a heavy dragon, so I was able to study him up close. His legs were as thick around as tree trunks, ending in serrated, knife-sharp claws. His wings were huge, and dark as night, since he was ink-black. His long muzzle had a Roman arch; I'd thought only humans could have a Roman nose. The gathering dragon reminded me of a bird. Zephyr was a mix of orange and blue, with a flare of skin behind his head, like a crest. His wings were feathered, unlike Stellar's bat wings. The feathers ran from sky blue, to turquoise, to navy. Meisha's dragon, Maath, was a perfect example of a typical messenger dragon. Maath was cloudy gray, with creamy white on his underside breaking it up. He had white freckles on his muzzle; Meisha explained that it was because he was a twin.

When dragons mated, excess eggs were laid; only one or two hatched. The extra eggs were decoys; most predators in the few places dragons lived in the wild didn't go after dragon eggs because of the extreme likelihood they wouldn't find anything. Even if they did, they would have an enormous, angry mother dragon to contend with. Twins were hatchlings that hatched out of the exact same egg. Something about their genetics changed their markings; unlike most dragons, which were solid colors that faded into darker or lighter, twins had spots or other markings.

Maath's twin was Eir. He was the opposite end of the gray spectrum, a stormy gray with jagged slashes of white like lightning bolts breaking through the clouds in the middle of a storm. He had splotches of light gray mixed in with the dark and white, making him look like a pinto pony. His rider was gone; I had no idea who he was. All I knew was that he was in the infirmary after his mission had gone wrong. Chase had been so ominous and evasive about it that it gave me a terrible feeling. He would say only that the mission had gone sideways. Of course that had piqued my interest, but no matter how much I pestered him, he refused to say anything more. Eventually I just gave up, with a mental note to ask about it later, when his guard was down. If it ever was.

"Go away," Syren said, his gentle tone belying the harsh words. I shook my head mid-yawn; I was exhausted, but refused to go to bed before the other riders. Two reasons: A. the stories they told were fascinating, and B. I was not going to seem weak in front of them. I considered protesting, but I thought my huge yawn probably gave it away. I stood, trying to preserve some dignity.

"I suppose," I said casually. I scooped up Stellar, who was pouncing on a piece of leftover broccoli like it had offended her ancestors. She gnawed on it even as I carried her. I didn't have the heart to take it away from her. Dragons are definitely like toddlers in that respect: you don't take their toys away from them, not unless you want to listen to them whine about it. And since dragons can whine in your head as well, it's doubly not a good idea.

Back in my room, I slithered out of my uniform, top first. I tossed it on the bed and slipped out of my pants, folding them carefully, along with my top. I placed the stack on the short stool parallel to my bed stand, then plopped down and unzipped my boots, standing them in front of the stool so my whole uniform was all together.

As it had been several days since Stellar had hatched, I'd been given my own room in the barracks. Unlike the name suggested, it wasn't one big communal living space, but rather split into rooms for each rider, with a few extras. It was small; I'm sure most prison cells were bigger, but it was ours. I put my pajamas on without thinking about it, a pair of loose gray sweats with Hockey written down the thigh and a ratty T-shirt.

I flopped onto my bed, careful not to flatten Stellar, who was fast asleep on her cushion. There was also a small nest on a pedestal in the corner, made of thick straw and shaped roughly like a football. It, and the pedestal it was on, had shown up the day after she'd hatched, not that it mattered. She totally ignored it. Honestly, I was lucky if she stayed on her cushion all night; most of the time I woke up with her on my chest or head, both of which could pose a serious issue when she started getting bigger. Her nose crinkled adorably while she slept. Possessed by a sudden impulse, I reached over and ran my forefinger from the top of her head all the way down her spine. My eyes closed, and I sank gratefully into the blackness. I was so tired I was unconscious by the time my head hit the pillow.

Chapter Eleven

The staff hit my finger, and my bruises screamed in protest. Three weeks after the start of my training, my body was covered with bruises and scrapes. I'd cut myself on knives, pinched fingers between staffs, and smacked myself with nunchucks. I'd fallen over barrels I had to jump over, with a jarring landing. My hands were burned red from climbing ropes. I'd been smacked mercilessly with wooden sticks as I crawled nets and climbed walls, by people standing on platforms or above me. And I'd never felt better.

As for my progress with Stellar, she was still working hard, but as far as I was concerned, I was ready for missions. My training was going great, and I had minimal trouble with both the mental and physical aspects of our task.

Stellar and I were closer together. Two weeks ago, Stellar, the size of a Labrador Retriever, had made her boldest advance into my mind yet. After a long day of training, I had been going through practice drills with a blunt knife, humming an old lullaby gently under my breath. Something about it sounded strange to me, like there was an echo. I heard the melody of the song twice, like there were two devices playing the same song simultaneously. I overlooked it at first, deciding I was just imagining it. I nearly fumbled the knife out of my hand and stabbed myself with it when I heard a clear, distinct voice in my head state, *I like it.*

Stellar had her head lifted; she wove back and forth like a snake being charmed. *I do too*, I returned cautiously. This lullaby had been the only one my mother had ever sung to me, and even this one only a few times, in moments of weakness.

To my shock, Stellar began to hum; it perfectly matched the melody I was humming. She sat up, tail wrapped around her ankles like a cat. *Good night*, she sent decisively. She leapt off my bed and onto her cushion, circling a few times before settling down.

I stared slack-jawed after her for a second, shook my head in wonder, and crawled into bed. I pulled my covers up to my chin, turned onto my side, and dropped my head onto my pillow. It felt like only an hour had passed before the alarm on my phone buzzed to wake me up, but I rolled out of bed and headed gamely to training, Stellar padding behind me like an enormous dog.

"You are being trained as a solo messenger," Hale began. He and Chase stood in the gym, looking extremely out of place. I'd heard that Chase trained, but never when I was there, which was pretty much all the time. I was almost entirely sure Hale hadn't trained for many years. Not that he was fat or anything, but I didn't expect someone that old to get up every morning and beat the crap out of a punching bag or kicking shield. Or a person, for that matter. I took a swig from my reusable bottle, trying to replenish some of the liquid I had lost with my ample sweating. The flavored energy drink soothed my dry throat and tongue in a blue wave.

"Yes," I agreed warily. He knew all this, and knew I knew, so where was he going with it? He'd told me to begin with. All that talk about teams, and Stellar and I were on our own. I didn't play well with others, so maybe it was just as well.

"But…" he hesitated. "For your first mission, we'd prefer you have back up, just in case. You and Stellar will be sent out first; the others will follow a few hours later. If you have any troubles, land and wait for them to catch up with you," he finished.

I felt a flush of displeasure. Didn't they trust me? If they didn't, why were they sending us out on a mission?

"Okay," I agreed reluctantly. "By the way, who are my teammates?" I stared at them askance. Chase seemed in a bad mood for some reason. He kept pulling on his collar and curling his lip at the people working out. Maybe it had been awhile since he'd worked out?

"Why?" Chase asked rudely. "Afraid we'll send you out with someone you dislike?"

Like you? Stellar observed darkly; I choked.

"No," I coughed, struggling to tamp down my laughter. "I'm only curious."

"We're sending Meisha and Orion," Hale said quietly, staring at Chase oddly too. "But first, we'll send you guys out on a test flight. It's the last step in your training."

"A week in the wild, with your dragon and your teammates, with minimal supplies," Chase said, with a little too much relish for my taste. "Can you do it?" he challenged.

I bristled. "Do you doubt it?" I glared at him. What was his problem? Stellar caught my mood; she rose up onto her hind legs, flaring her wings and hissing a warning. It didn't matter how well she knew them; if someone upset me, they'd have a very upset dragon to deal with.

Step off, buddy, she rumbled in my mind. My temple throbbed painfully. I struggled not to snap. Stellar's anger was amplifying mine, making it far worse. I swallowed thickly, praying she'd cool down. Sooner rather than later.

Hale intervened. "Of course we don't," he soothed. "Also, it will be necessary that you fly out into the wilds where you are staying. One of your teammates will explain to you the particulars," he explained. "They have both done this before."

"Alright," I agreed. "I'll catch up with them when I'm finished."

I set down my water bottle, picking up my staff with a pointed remark that I still had to complete my training for the day. Hale and Chase bowed out; I think Hale was relieved to have a good excuse. Chase stalked out ahead of him and I made a face at his retreating back. Stellar chimed, the sound more like the bells in a church tower than the tinkling handhelds that it had once sounded like.

Every day, a clipboard with our name on it was placed on a hook just inside the gym door. Sometime during the day you had to complete the list it detailed. It specified exercises, number of reps, laps, etc. If you didn't finish it, not only did you have to add it to the next day's work out, you had to run a set amount of laps on the indoor running track. It was placed high overhead; the dragons often perched there, making it an exercise in dodging as much as a run.

Smack! I panted quietly, my long staff raised against my training partner's vulnerable throat. He lay on his back on the blue training mat; his own staff lay some feet away.

"That's enough," David called. I stepped away, flicking my staff back into carrying position. I extended my free hand to help my opponent up from the mat.

"Not bad," he approved. "It's always nice to have a challenge." My training partner stepped away as David's huge form lumbered over to us.

"Your training is going well," he rumbled. "You're ready for everything I can train you for." He reached into one of his deep cargo pockets. His uniform was different from mine, a long sleeved athletic top with olive green cargo pants that had more pockets than I'd ever seen in my entire life.

He tugged out a pen from another pocket. His huge hands looked strange holding such a delicate item. Huh. Never thought I'd describe a fifty cent ballpoint as 'delicate'.

He scrawled his signature on the paper, which was crumpled and had a jagged rip down one corner that was surrounded by what looked to be fang marks. There was an unidentifiable stain in the top right corner as well. The poor thing looked like it had survived a war - barely.

"This is my sign-off that you're ready to go on your training mission," he explained. "But I'm giving you one last thing."

He strolled over to a knife rack, gesturing that I was to follow him. We had racks like this all over the gym; I didn't get what was so special about this particular one. Knives of all shapes and sizes were cradled on their hooks, sheathed. I was sure if you unsheathed them they would be gleaming and ready. Six rows of six apiece, thirty-six total. There were other racks as well: a tall one balancing staffs, and one holding swords. A wicker bin on the floor contained fans, some laced with blades and others without. A wide rack had quivers full of arrows hanging on its hooks, bows in their cases beneath that.

He bent over and reached behind the rack. He straightened up with a package wrapped in canvas and tied with twine. His expression was almost shy as he proffered it.

"Whenever a student of mine graduates, I give them a weapon that fits them, so they'll never be without," he said quietly. "Open it."

I did, carefully loosening the twine and slipping the canvas away. A dagger lay inside. The sheath was deep black, etched with letters outlined in indigo, my favorite color. The ribbed indigo-and-black-grip of the hilt was wrapped in leather. I tightened my hand around it and pulled; the dagger left its sheath with barely a whisper. It fit in my hand like it was made for me, which, if I really thought about it, it might have been. It was single-bladed and made of gleaming steel that shone in even the dim lighting of the workout area, narrowing to a needle-point. When I looked more closely, I could see a symbol pressed into the blade; some kind of flower. The name for it popped into my head so suddenly I wondered if it came from Stellar: *fleur-de-lis*.

"This is a stiletto," David began. "It's been a very popular weapon for hundreds of years. It fits you better than others, I think. Classier, I guess. I hope you like it."

"Thank you," I said, sincerely touched. I couldn't believe that he had taken time out of his busy day to search this out for me. Plus, it seemed to be antique, or at the very least handmade; it couldn't have been cheap. If he did this for all of his students, how much money had he spent over the years to equip graduating students?

"You're welcome." He placed his hand on my shoulder, squeezing gently as he walked in the opposite direction to answer a question.

I decided to speak to my teammates in the morning. Tomorrow was a big day; Stellar was being moved to The Loft. A new one had been built, as we needed the room for the new dragons. We'd be moved into the new one, which made me all the more leery of going on a trip out in the middle of nowhere. If I got used to living in the lap of luxury, how much harder would it be?

Chapter Twelve

"Hey, wait up!" I called, jogging quickly to catch up. My dagger bounced against my hip. Meisha turned, startled. His eyes widened slightly when he saw me, but the look vanished as quickly as it had come.

"Yes?" he asked, puzzled.

I panted quietly, taking deep breaths and holding up one finger for him to wait. I had never been a good runner. It seemed that weeks of strenuous training had done little to change that.

"Hale said I needed to speak with you," I started. "You're one of my teammates for my training mission; you're supposed to explain it to me more?" It was meant as a statement, but it came out like a question.

"Oh!" he said, seeming to realize it only now. "Yeah. We can talk over breakfast. You were going to breakfast, right?" he asked cautiously, when he saw me hesitate.

Confession time. I had been a hockey player for years; it had done wonders for my confidence. When I was younger, though, I had been a lot less athletic. I was a bookworm; I enjoyed curling up inside with a good book more than anything else, no matter the weather. I wasn't fat, but my weight was... oddly distributed. My mother, the doctor, took it upon herself to tell me, in not-so-gentle terms, that my weight was out of control. Believe me, it's one thing for someone to call you fat, as an insult, and a whole 'nother for your own mother to tell you. She threatened to put me on a diet if I didn't lose weight and get down to what she called "a proper size." Since then, I'd been very sensitive about my weight.

One of the things that a dragon changed about a rider was our appetite. I was hungry all the time now, and had the metabolism to go with it. We riders ate huge meals several times a day, yet you wouldn't find a chubby one among us. Tall and lean, we rippled with muscles. It felt like a dream come true, but I was terrified that one day it would all come crashing down, that I'd be fat again. I wasn't a fanatic, but I did skip a meal occasionally. My own way of not jinxing it, I guess.

"Yeah," I answered. I hadn't planned to eat today, but I couldn't exactly refuse. He had an odd expression on his face.

"Are we going, or what?" He snapped out of it, smiling sheepishly and motioning politely for me to go ahead of him.

We stepped into the main house, where every rider ate meals. We ate in shifts, so we didn't fill up the kitchen. You would not believe the amount of food we can eat. The kitchen was never empty, as riders came in early and late. By the time one meal was finished, another was about to begin.

I scooped a sausage onto my plate. It was already filled with two slices of toast, a heap of scrambled eggs, thick strips of bacon, pancakes, and a blueberry muffin. A half-peeled pomegranate balanced against my full glass of orange juice, my only attempt at a healthy food for this meal.

"Hey," Orion said suddenly. I glanced up, mouth full. "I didn't know you were left-handed." I gulped a piece of sausage down my suddenly dry throat, and the sip of orange juice I took did little to soothe it.

"I'm not," I responded. "I'm ambidextrous, and I hurt my shoulder recently. Still favoring it, I guess." I flexed my shoulder, feeling only the slightest twinge. I'd stopped wearing my sling the week after I'd arrived, when I suddenly didn't feel like I didn't need it anymore. Another benefit of being a dragon rider. Dragons were so rarely injured, because of their diamond hard scales, that their riders healed far faster than any normal person could. Three cheers for sharing, I guess.

"Cool," Meisha observed.

"When did you hurt your shoulder? How?" Orion asked, face inscrutable. His nose was wrinkled, which made his constellation stand out vividly.

"Hockey," I shrugged, not sure why it was such a big deal. He dropped it, but he still had a strange expression on his face.

"Soo…" Meisha said, drawing the word out as he glanced between the two of us. "We needed to talk about the trip?"

"Yes," I confirmed. Orion looked puzzled, which puzzled me. Hadn't Hale told him he'd be one of my teammates? "You and Orion are supposed to be my teammates."

"Yeah. So we'll pack, fly down there, stay for a week and come back. We'll wait a while before we leave, just to make totally sure that Stellar can fly with your weight," he explained.

"Hale said something about me leaving early?" I checked.

Meisha nodded. "As this is your trip, you'll leave a few hours before us; we'll catch up to you and fly back together."

I nodded. "Okay." I went back to shoveling food in my mouth, starting with bacon. When I'd finished, I scooped up my utensils, plate, and glass, then carried the pile into the kitchen. I dumped my breakfast things into the sink and washed my hands at the faucet since I'd gotten syrup on my hand when I reached for my glass.

Orion came up behind me. "Are you sure you're ready for this?"

I frowned thunderously. "Why does everyone keep asking me that? Do *you* think I'm ready?" I asked, turning the question around on him. I wasn't sure whether to be hurt or angry that apparently no one here believed in me.

He threw his hands up in comic surrender and sighed. "Of course I do," he assured. "I'm just checking. Would you like me to accompany you to training?"

"Sure," I agreed, secretly relieved. It helped somehow, to know that he did believe in me, even just a little. "But I'll have to leave early. Stellar and I are moving to the new Loft today."

He held the door open for me, which surprised me. Apparently, chivalry isn't dead. Or, at least not among riders, who were the only people I could remember holding the door in recent past.

We walked out of the training arena. I half-turned to wave goodbye to my training partner of the day. After two hours of training, I was bathed in sweat, and was hoping for a real shower before I had to move into the Loft. It hadn't taken me long to complete my training. Twenty laps, a twenty-minute knife session, and a run-through of the obstacle course. It had been fun, despite the throb of bruises and the protesting of my muscles. The knife session was the best, since I was able to use my new stiletto as well as the throwing knives that I was so proficient with. Said dagger swung at my waist, the sheath clipped onto the belt of my uniform, in a sort of niche that Madame LaVarne had left for it. I'd been told that it would be easier to have the knife in my boot while flying to reduce the risk of losing it, but I wasn't flying yet, so I was content.

I stepped out of the shower, wrapped in a thick towel. My long brown hair hung in limp strings, dripping beads of water onto my pale skin. I dried myself hurriedly, because I was supposed to carry my things down to the new Loft soon. The Loft was housing for both dragons and their riders. There were several doors, in the ceiling and at the ground, so it was convenient for all of us. The raised platforms our dragons slept on, we slept on as well. It was a daily trust exercise: Pray you don't roll off, or pray your dragon is awake enough to rescue you if you do.

It took quite a while to move my things into the new loft, not so much because I had lots of things to carry, because I didn't. It was more because of the fact that there were so many others coming in as well. It felt like what I imagined college move in day would be like, with everyone tripping over each other because they couldn't see over their boxes and bickering about who got which spots. College felt like an unattainable dream, but I wouldn't have traded Stellar and my new friends for anything in the world.

Comfortable? Stellar asked. We lay on our platform, getting ready to sleep for the night. I leaned against Stellar's shoulder, careful to avoid the spikes; one wing was wrapped around me. Her tail curled protectively around my ankles. Stellar did that all the time; apparently most dragons didn't. I'd laughed so hard when another rider asked me about it. He was claustrophobic, so when his dragon wrapped his ankles with her tail, he'd nearly screamed. He told me it made him feel like he was tied up. How would he know?

Very. Good night.

Stellar stretched her neck up over my head, which was tilted back. She touched my forehead with her muzzle, swiping over it gently with her tongue for good measure. *Good night, Ax.*

Chapter Thirteen

Something poked me. I cracked one eye, ready to tell Stellar off. Instead, I came face to face with Meisha. Too close. I scrambled away, crab-crawling until my back hit the wall. Stellar lifted her head sleepily, disturbed only because I wasn't under her wing.

"Dude, too close," I gasped.

He flushed sheepishly. "Sorry. I just wanted to tell you it was time to get up." Orion popped his head over the edge of our platform. It took me a moment to realize that he was probably standing on Tyne's back.

"Yep," Orion seconded. He dropped suddenly; I heard his startled yelp and Tyne's rumble of laughter. Meisha glanced over his shoulder to check on him, his lips twisting as he struggled not to laugh.

"You okay?" he called down. I heard Orion's muffled affirmation; he sounded grumpy.

Orion popped back up. "Not a word," he warned.

"Of course not," I said, completely poker-faced, even though Stellar's mental laughter made it extremely difficult to stay that way. "Now go away so I can get dressed."

I shooed Meisha off the platform. Stellar turned toward the wall, rising on her hind legs and flaring her wings. It was the dragon equivalent of a screen, which was all the privacy we'd get in the loft. I snatched my uniform and dragged it on as quickly as I could, my fumbling fingers buckling the straps incorrectly. I huffed under my breath, but slowed down enough to fix them. I buckled my dagger on, careful to make sure it hung correctly. If it didn't, it dug into my thigh, which was painful when I sat. Stellar stepped to the side and lay back down while I put my boots on; the boys peeked at me. I zipped my boots and crawled onto Stellar's back, settling myself between her spikes.

"What's up today?" I asked eagerly. For the past few days we'd been preparing for our trip, gathering the necessities. Clothes, food, and such, along with a few weapons.

"Saddles," Orion answered, earning a mutinous glare from Meisha, who'd had his mouth open to answer my question. "You need one. Stellar needs to be measured before they can make it."

"Okay," I said, though I was actually a little disappointed. Saddles? Seriously? Boring.

Stellar was far more patient with being measured than I would have been. She stood still as a statue while they measured her. Around her stomach, chest, and throat, then along her back and wings. Two women took care of everything. The brunette did the measuring; the blonde wrote down her measurements on a green clipboard. When they weren't working on her, I was rubbing down her wings and shining her scales. As a young dragon grows, their scales get thinner and eventually fall off, to be replaced by the diamond hard scales that typified the adult dragons. Stellar was in that in-between stage where they needed to be buffed and shone in order to strengthen them and remove the excess. I was careful to stay out of the ladies' way while they were measuring her, but taking care of Stellar was taking more and more time these days, and I wasn't one to waste any time to do that.

"Should be done in a few days," the brunette decided, in her surprisingly deep voice. "Come back then."

"That's it?" I complained outside. The boys laughed.

"Relax," Orion soothed. "We'll leave soon enough. We'll be ready before you know it."

Chapter Fourteen

"First aid kit," Orion called. I dug through the pile at my feet, coming up with a travel-size white box, the red cross standing out brightly.

"Got it," I responded. He checked it off the clipboard he held, and searched again, pen poised. His tongue peeked out the corner of his lips in concentration, which I thought was hilarious. I used to have that same habit, until I started playing hockey. When you're told, by more than one person, that you could bite your tongue off even with a mouth guard, you drop it real quick.

"Matches?" I found the long, rectangular box fairly easily. Most people would have used a lighter, even for camping, but I understood why the matches. Unless you get them wet, matches are good; you don't have to worry about them running out of fuel and refusing to light. Meisha tossed a coil of rope to me, obviously anticipating Orion's next request, and Orion checked it off the list without comment.

"Flashlight and/or lantern?" Orion read off. I pulled an LED lantern and a round blue flashlight out of the mound and set them off to the side.

"And... navigation carton." I tilted my head, puzzled. Meisha found that one, a rectangular, weatherproof, green box. Meisha unlatched it quickly, displaying the contents: a beat-up compass with a crooked needle and a stack of laminated maps.

"So we don't get lost," Meisha explained.

I gave him a dry look. "So I gathered from 'navigation'." He flushed bull-rag red.

We separated the supplies into knapsacks and saddlebags. Two knapsacks and saddlebags apiece, each with emergency supplies, like food and a satellite phone, since the wilds were far out of range of any cell tower.

"When do we leave?" I asked, practically bouncing with enthusiasm. Stellar echoed me, her keenness to go ringing through the inquiry. Her wings rippled and her legs tensed in preparation for flight.

"Soon," Orion hedged. I huffed indignantly.

"Cop-out," I complained. Stellar rumbled a laugh, her chest vibrating against my shoulders. The boys grinned playfully and shrugged in unison. "Fine," I grumbled. "I'm going for a ride."

"With your new saddle?" Orion teased, throwing my complaint back in my face.

"Yes," I responded, refusing to react. I had complained about the time it took to make the saddle, time I had considered 'wasted', but now I was glad that we'd taken that time. I stalked off with Stellar, the boy's laughter ringing in my ears as I strode in the opposite direction.

My saddle, or rather, Stellar's, was a thing of beauty. It was tanned leather, shaped like a cross between a horse saddle and one used on a camel, which was an odd combination. Black fleur-de-lis were burnt into the leather, standing out starkly against the fawn. A broad strap emblazoned with more fleur-de-lis crossed Stellar's chest and buckled on the other side; the design was also on the cinch that tightened around her belly. The saddle sat further forward than most, to accommodate her wings.

I pulled on my riding jacket. Madame LaVarne had made it for me as soon as she'd heard I was receiving a saddle. Dragons flew at extremely high altitudes, and their frail human riders couldn't handle the blistering cold at those heights. Madame LaVarne had perfected the art of designing our riding jackets; they were both warm and stylish. Mine was black leather, with thin turquoise and indigo stripes on the shoulders and biceps. A big indigo fleur-de-lis was ringed with turquoise in the middle of my back. Paired with my tan saddle, accented with black, we cut quite a striking figure, if I do say so myself.

I tightened the straps around my long legs. Stellar jittered impatiently beneath me.

"I know, I know," I laughed, tugging to ensure the knot was tight. Straps on the saddle at my knees, calves, and ankles kept me in the saddle when Stellar decided to do some fancy aerial maneuver with no warning. Dragons are like that.

"Ready," I told her. *About time*, she grumped, but I could hear the undercurrent of humor in her thought. She crouched and raised her wings high above her head, muscles tightening. She lunged, sweeping her huge black wings down in a deep scoop to catch the air. Her neck weaved as she gained altitude, and my cheeks flushed from the chill. The fleece lining of my riding jacket protected my torso, and my pants protected my legs, but where was protection for my face? I resolved to complain to Madame LaVarne later.

"Woo-hoo!" I yelled. My throat scraped painfully; I coughed, but couldn't hide my ecstatic grin. My braid flew back from my face as the wind whipped. I leaned low over Stellar's neck, uncomfortably close to her gray spikes. *This. Is. Awesome!*

If you think watching sunsets in general is beautiful, you should see it from dragon-back. On the ground, you see maybe one or two colors as the sun sinks below the horizon. From up here, I could see the sun itself, surrounded by a radiant halo of carnelian, blush pink, maroon, and russet red. The air was chill; my breath fogged in the air. My cheeks stung from the wind.

It's beautiful, Stellar decided contentedly. I heartily agreed. It saddened me a little to realize that on our training trip, this probably wouldn't be an option. Orion and Meisha would almost definitely not be impressed if we went flying only to see the sunset. I rolled ideas over in my mind as Stellar banked to head back, and contrived to think of an excuse for an evening flight.

From above, it was easy to see everything. As we swooped lazily over the grounds, I could pick out anyone who was outside. There were a few dragons wheeling in the air over the lake, and a few more splashing around, sending up gouts of clear water as they dove into the water. Small groups of riders were clustered together, some walking with their dragons and some just walking together. Two tiny figures stood behind one of the barns. Something about their body language seemed off, as if they were hiding, or just didn't want to be seen. I squinted, and asked Stellar to fly a little lower, purely out of curiosity. She angled her wings and dove, using her thick tail to steer. They couldn't see us, but I could see just the one facing out; the other had their back to me, and I didn't dare have Stellar drop any lower for fear that they would see us. The one facing us was... Hale. His silver hair shone in the sun, and his hands whipped in the air as he gestured wildly. The other man had dark hair and was tall, but that was all the detail I could make out. Unsatisfied and curious, I asked Stellar to fly away, and tried to push it out of my mind.

My boots thudded onto the ground, sending up a puff of dust. I walked into the loft, absentmindedly scratching under Stellar's chin. From the top of her neck, down over her chest, and under to her stomach was cloudy gray; she loved to be scratched there for some reason. Her chest vibrated as she purred. It sounded a bit like a very, very large cat, but deeper and more rhythmic. I carefully pulled off her saddle, loosening the straps and pulling it over her back, and my arms shook from the effort. Some parts of a dragon's scales were sharp; the material of their saddles was thicker to accommodate it. It was heavier than you'd expect.

First order of business: brush Stellar. And no, not like a horse. A dragon's scales need to be scrubbed every day with a wire brush to bring out the glow. The first few days, my hands had been red and chapped; it had gotten better as I learned. I also had gloves now, fingerless ones that Madame LaVarne had made me to replace the ratty ones in the trunk. It hurt less to use the wire brush when I had them on.

See, every rider has a daily regimen for their dragon. In the morning, I got up, made Stellar's meal, heated it, and gave it to her. She didn't like it too hot, but not too cold either; it had to be warm, and warm only. While she ate, I cleaned her stall, layering another level of straw, moss, and bracken. That's most of our routine there. The rest is at the end of the day. I brushed her, cleaned around her eyes with a soft cloth, and oiled her wings. Years ago, dragon riders had discovered a specific mixture that, when combined carefully and applied daily, made a dragon's wings flexible and resilient. The ingredients for the mix were extremely hard to come by, so we used it sparingly. It was practically a sin to waste it, although no one I knew ever did.

Stellar leaned into the brush; I scrubbed harder, digging into the nooks and crannies. My arms ached as I pressed, but she'd once told me it was like getting your back scratched, only much, much better. I could manage it for a little while longer. She sighed darkly when I pulled it away and glared, her slit green eyes flashing.

I was done, I defended. She huffed, but her lips peeled back from her sharp teeth in an approximation of a smile. I battered down a shiver. It was meant as a compliment, but all those razor-sharp white teeth made me nervous.

I know.

I reached into the kit at my feet, similar to a horse's grooming bucket, and pulled out a small cloth. I rubbed it carefully in the corners of Stellar's eyes, picking out the crust. Her eyes crossed, which was hilarious; the snake-like eyes dilated. She reared up slightly, trying to balance herself. *Stop that*, I chided, trying not to laugh. She huffed, but thumped back down, right next to me. I didn't move; I knew she wouldn't land on me. Not on purpose anyway.

I made sure my foot was steady on the rung before I put my weight on it. I climbed down, rung by rung, jumping off with three left, flexing my knees to keep from pitching forward or backward. I jogged into the side room and reached, dragging a clear glass vial off the shelf that ran the expanse of the room. I stuck it in my cargo pocket before I started climbing back up the ladder.

Stellar was asleep on our platform when I reached it. I yawned wistfully, wanting to lie down and sleep too, but I couldn't, not just yet. I tugged lightly on Stellar's right wing; she twitched it out with a grumble. I pulled the stopper out of the bottle, wiping off the tiny sponge-brush before I slowly began applying it to her wing.

It took me half an hour to oil Stellar's huge wings. They shone like onyx as I sat back and surveyed my work. I grudgingly admitted that it was worth the work, even though I was exhausted. It took me another few minutes to go up and down the maze of ladders and reach our perch. I glanced over at my boots, and knew I should oil them. The black was scuffed; Madame LaVarne would take a chunk out of me if she knew I'd left them like this. I went back and forth, trying to decide if I should or not. Did I have time?

Do it in the morning, Stellar grumped. I grinned, realizing my inner turmoil had kept her awake. *Sorry,* I sent, falsely sheepish. She gave me the cold shoulder as I lay down, refusing to let me sleep under her wing like I typically did. It was freezing in here, so I retrieved my blankets and laid down. The lights blinked off abruptly, but I was already half asleep.

My eyes blinked open, but it wasn't any lighter once I did. Dragons were extremely photosensitive when tired, so the loft was pitch black at night. That might not be a problem when you're asleep, but when you need to climb down several ladders to even reach the floor it is not pleasant. Plus, our bathrooms were a quarter of a mile away, in a dingy little building that served as both our shower house and our restrooms. If you even thought you might need to use the restroom, it's best to go; by the time you get there, you definitely will.

I fumbled for my flashlight, trying to clip it to my belt and dim it to the lowest light setting before it woke anyone else up. I groped around for my boots. Where had I left them? I could have sworn I'd left them over in the corner… ah, there they were. Dragons shed claws and scales like little kids lose teeth, so you never, ever walk around the loft barefooted, especially not in the dark. If you think stepping on kid's toy pieces is bad, imagine stepping on the razor-sharp scale of an adolescent dragon. I shuddered just thinking about it. I placed my feet carefully on the rungs of the ladder as I climbed down; I was on my own. Stellar hadn't even twitched, physically or in the shared space of our minds, when I had asked her to carry me down to the floor.

I scrubbed my hands carefully, squinting in the bright light of the bathroom. It was fine in the light of day, but we riders were photosensitive too; in the murky, smoggy darkness of the grounds, the bright incandescent light stood out like a lantern fish in the darkest trench of the ocean. I pushed the slatted door of the bathhouse open carefully and reached back inside to flick off the light switch.

I stepped around the corner of the loft, and froze. I reeled back, pressing my shoulders against the wall around the corner. *What the crap?* I carefully peeked around the corner, trying to adjust to what I was seeing. A svelte, bottle blonde teenage girl leaned casually against the wall, arms crossed. She wasn't alone. Orion had his hands pressed into the building on either side of her shoulders, leaning his face toward hers. I could see his lips moving; she responded. I padded away, attempting to keep my boots from crunching on the gravel. Maybe they were talking now, but judging by their body language, they wouldn't be soon. Better to give them their privacy, whoever she was.

Chapter Fifteen

S tellar twitched; her wing swished into my back. I flinched, trying to keep my attention forward. Hale was speaking, explaining to everyone that my partners and I would be off on my training trip for a while, and not to worry if we weren't available. Stellar buried her nose between my shoulder blades and rasped it up and down; I went rigid.

What is your problem? I hissed. She threw her head up in agitation.

I have something in my eye, she whined. I saw her raise her paw toward her face, all five sharp claws flashing.

"Don't!" I blurted, louder than I'd intended. Heads swiveled, but the great thing about riders is they know all about having conversations with "yourself." When other people would have had you admitted to a mental institution, they didn't bat an eye. "Does anyone have a cloth?" I asked sheepishly. "Stellar has something in her eye and I left mine in the barn."

Cloths popped up everywhere, and I was reminded ridiculously of knights being offered a lady's favor. "Thanks," I mumbled, flushed bright red. A girl smiled sympathetically.

"We've all been there," she whispered soothingly. She patted my arm and handed me her handkerchief; the impatient wave of her hand sent the others back into conversation like nothing had happened.

We all filed out to where our dragons waited patiently. Orion,

Meisha, and I went through our bags one more time, checking yet again that we had everything we needed. Clothes, food, water, the whole shebang. I also ensured that I had my dagger and whetstone. The dagger was sheathed tightly in the pocket in my boot, freshly polished and sharpened. I'd done it right after I'd polished my boots, actually.

"Bye!" the other riders chorused. Orion and Meisha were at the front of the crowd, but any assurances or advice they may have had were lost in the cheers and well-wishing from behind them. I tightened the last strap on my saddle, waving as Stellar launched upward. Her wings snapped downward, sweeping air.

Stellar and I had fun. We took off earlier than the others, so we had plenty of time to think. She swooped and dove, twisting into complex aerial maneuvers that had me hanging on for dear life and checking the straps to make sure they were tight. Stellar laughed at me, but as much as my butt hurt, I didn't particularly want to land the hard way.

The scenery was beautiful. Tall, straight pine trees reached for the skies, deep green needles stretched out to the sides like they were trying to hold hands. Stellar glided through a robin's egg blue sky, floating through the clouds. The sun beat down, warm enough that I peeled off my riding jacket and shoved it into my saddlebag, folded at the top so that I could reach it easily if I needed it. Then I twisted back around, inhaling a deep breath of fresh air. From our vantage point in the sky, we could see everything for miles.

I received quite the fright when Stellar decided she was hungry mid-flight and went after a rabbit. She flattened her wings to her sides and plummeted toward the ground, nose first. At the very last second, only a few feet above the ground, she flared her wings hugely, stretching them up and out so that they caught the wind. She pounced on an enormous hare, snapping its neck easily. *I'm off*, I mumbled; I swallowed hard. My fingers fumbled to release the straps that held me to the saddle. *Okay.*

Too-large shadows on the ground startled me. Maath and Tyne swooped down slowly, circling like hawks. I stared at their shadows on the ground, watching them shrink and enlarge respectively. Apparently they hadn't been as far behind as I'd thought.

"What happened?" Orion asked worriedly. I waved my hand loosely at Stellar, gulping the rabbit and a deer she'd brought down, behind me. Both Orion's and Meisha's faces relaxed immediately. They unstrapped too, and the dragons padded off into the forest, presumably to hunt.

Sorry, Stellar sent sheepishly. *I was hungry.* She crawled forward and settled down at my back, her warm exhalations lifting the hair at the nape of my neck. I could feel her muzzle hanging in the air over my shoulder.

I relented. *It's fine. A little warning next time, though?*

Definitely, she agreed, eager for forgiveness.

"On that note, time for lunch," I said aloud. Orion dug through his saddlebag, coming up with military-style fire cooked meals. We gathered tinder and stones to make a pit; we had to call Tyne, the more easygoing of the dragons, to light it. Stellar grumbled about not being able to breathe fire yet, and I soothed her. We dropped the food into a pan and held it over the fire, waiting patiently for it to cook.

We ladled the food carefully into foam bowls. It was a bit of a balancing act: if you took too long, you'd get burnt, which I found out the hard way.

"Flipping ouch!" I barked, flapping my burnt hand to get a little air on it. It was bright red in the center of my palm, overlapping both calluses and blisters.

Meisha was at my side in an instant. "Are you okay?" he asked worriedly. Orion went for the first aid kit, but I waved him off.

"I'm fine." At their identical disbelieving looks, I hurried to assure them. "I swear. But y'all can serve your own food." I stepped away from the fire with my food, trying to hide how much it hurt.

The boys nodded fervently. "We can do that."

Stellar dipped her muzzle toward my shoulder and sniffed my hand. *Ouch*, she observed. She swept her tongue gently over it, again and again. The burn shrank, but it would be a while before it stopped hurting.

Thank you.

I swallowed my food, if you could call it that, before I spoke. "So when will we reach the site?" I asked. Everyone used the same site for their training trip, just in case something happened. If someone disappeared or was seriously injured, they knew exactly where to look. As the others had already done the trip several times, they knew where we were headed. I didn't.

Orion considered. "Tomorrow?" he guessed, glancing to Meisha for confirmation. Meisha nodded, shoveling another spoonful of doughy noodles into his mouth. I wasn't really all that sure of what it was supposed to be, exactly.

"We'll land just before the sun sets," Orion explained, banking the fire. I helped Meisha repack the bags while we waited for the dragons to return. Stellar napped, content and lazy from the food. I felt exactly the same.

Maath and Tyne padded into the clearing. They stood at attention while their riders loaded up, clipping the saddle bags into place. We all leapt into our saddles and strapped in. We did one last run-through to make sure we'd collected everything and that the fire was indeed out.

"Up we go!" I called cheerfully. I honestly didn't have any idea why I was that happy. We had hours of flying yet to go today, with another full day of riding tomorrow. My backside was both numb and aching; our saddles were comfortable, but not that comfortable. I had a sneaking suspicion that did nothing to dull my good mood, that the contentedness was because of Stellar. If your dragon is happy, so are you. If they aren't, you're not, no matter your own feelings.

"I'm so tired," I moaned. My entire body was stiff from sitting in the same position all day; my tailbone felt like it was about to detach. The boys looked at each other and burst out laughing. "Stop laughing at me!" I blurted indignantly.

Orion couldn't stop laughing. "We're not laughing at you," he gasped. "It's just very different from how you were acting this morning."

"You're right, it is," I conceded with dignity. "And now I'm going to be even more different: I'm going to sleep."

I flapped out my sleeping bag, stretching out on the ground. *Moping isn't good*, Stellar observed. I sighed internally. *I know, but I'm too tired to deal with them right now.*

You are going to apologize in the morning?

Possibly, I admitted. She leveled one bright green eye at me; if she'd had eyebrows, they'd have been arched. *Fine! Yes, I'll apologize.*

"Good night," I threw out grumpily.

"Good night," Orion said laughingly, quietly echoed by Meisha.

Stellar curled loosely around my sleeping bag, extending her long neck so that her head was parallel with mine. She licked my forehead gently, pasting my sweaty hair to my forehead. *Dark, dear one,* she sent tenderly. *Sleep well. I'll be here in the morning.*

Chapter Sixteen

I never saw it coming. When I reflect on how different my life could have been if it hadn't happened, for good or ill, I come up with the same thing every time: I never saw it coming.

A hand clamped over my mouth; my instincts kicked in before I was fully awake. I thrust my elbow back, hard, and was answered by a soft grunt. I bit down viciously on the hand over my mouth, feeling bone crunch between my teeth. *Crack! Crack!* Gunshots ricocheted around the clearing. Something hit my body, in my stomach and shoulder. I felt like I'd been hit by a brick wall. Dragons screamed and the boys yelled; my world was tilting like I was on a roller coaster. *Stay up!* Stellar lunged toward me. One of her wings hung tattered and dripped with blood, all shredded muscle and tendons; she couldn't have taken off if she wanted.

Meisha slumped unconscious on Maath, who growled and snapped to keep soldiers at bay; there was a lot of blood, enough for me to know that if he wasn't dead yet, he would be soon. His upper chest appeared to be the source of the blood; his arm hung at his side, blood trickling down it and off his fingertips, splashing into a dark, ominous puddle on the forest floor. Orion was already mounted; Tyne had similar injuries to Stellar. Orion gripped his shoulder, blood dripping from his clawed hand.

A man stalked toward me. I lashed out, trying to kick him; my leg felt like it was filled with lead. He caught my ankle, holding it to his chest. Fine. If I couldn't hurt him, I was at least going to find out who he was. I gathered my depleted energy and shot my hand out, grabbed the mask, and ripped it off. Startled blue eyes stared at me; under the shock of raven-black hair, I realized that he was only my age. One of his high cheekbones was marred by a thin scar, faded white by the passage of time. His lips were rose-hip pink, full and arched like a bow. That hair cascaded over one royal blue eye, framed by girlishly long lashes that dusted his cheekbones when he blinked. Something about him seemed very familiar, but at the moment, I didn't have the energy to comb through every trivial interaction with a black haired boy that I'd ever had.

He stood at Stellar's shoulder, even as she snarled in his face; I was begrudgingly impressed at his bravery. He had no way of knowing it was a bluff, that Stellar wouldn't be able to breathe fire for a long time to come. He sucked in a breath and let out an earsplitting whistle that made me flinch. Stellar jittered to the side, startled. The boy still had my ankle, so it didn't get to come with me. I swallowed nausea. I felt like I was being drawn and quartered. Stellar was too wound up to realize the problem, but the boy wasn't. He released my ankle immediately, leaving it to flop against Stellar's side and startling her again.

The chaos ceased before the echo of the whistle had faded. Three soldiers held Orion in place by his arms, even though he struggled. I urged Stellar toward the boy, who'd turned away to see Orion and Meisha, just to see what he'd do. Guns swiveled to point toward us; the boy turned slowly.

"It's okay," he soothed. "Just come with us. All of you will be okay." He glanced back at Orion, who'd managed to wrench one arm free and elbow one of the soldiers in the jaw.

"Fine irony," I sneered. "What reason have we got to trust you? You ambushed, shot us, and might have killed him." I thrust my finger out and pointed toward Meisha, still unconscious on his injured dragon's back; his gray t-shirt was saturated with blood.

He flushed darkly and bit his lip. "This wasn't how it was supposed to go. If you hadn't struggled, we'd be back at Base. We have a trailer we use to transport injured… operatives." His hesitation, like he'd nearly slipped up, caught my attention even though my temple pounded to my heartbeat.

"We are not your operatives," I spat, anger flaring. Stellar's fury magnified my own considerable anger; my vision tunneled. I knew it was over.

Spots in all the colors of the spectrum did the cancan at the edges of my vision. I trembled, struggling to stay upright; blood oozed from at least two bullet wounds, if not more. I realized too late, not that there was anything I could have done about it before, that I was about to pass out from blood loss. I had only one thought as I keeled over: *Way to be a leader. Get yourself killed on a training mission.*

Cobalt

I lunged to catch the girl as she tumbled off her dragon. The dragon, an immense black female who looked older than I'd been told, snarled in my face; I froze. I had no great desire to be eaten. I folded my long legs carefully under me and settled to the ground, laying the girl half across my knees and balanced against my chest. I carefully freed one hand from behind the backs of her knees and raised it to the dragon in supplication. Her mental walls were unforgiving and solid as the door of a bank safe, and I couldn't have soothed her even if I'd wanted.

One of the men holding the boy, the one with the odd birthmark, peeled himself away from the gaggle. Perry, a trained field medic. He crouched next to me, carefully peeling up her pale eyelids. The startling green eyes I'd seen earlier were rolled up in her head, to the whites.

I swung my head back toward the boy. "What's her name?" I asked, my tone brooking no argument. The boy glared and tilted his head back, sneering down his nose. Anger flared, which, even from miles away, my dragon felt and mirrored, for no other reason than that I was feeling it. *Do you need me to join you?* he asked, immediately alert. I felt him raise his head and rustle his wings, readying for flight if necessary. *No!* I said, more sharply than was strictly necessary. *I can handle it.* He grumbled, but stretched back out, eyes open and clear.

I motioned for Perry to take the girl from my lap, and he did so, rather apprehensively. I lunged to my feet and stalked toward the boy. His magnificent blue dragon was already muzzled. I felt a twinge of sadness, and sympathy. I didn't particularly care about the riders except, strangely, the leader, but I did feel bad that the dragons had been injured. It was necessary; if we hadn't done it they'd have eaten us when we attacked, but that didn't mean I had to like it.

I grabbed a fistful of the boy's shirt and yanked him off his blue, who snarled weakly and trailed flame from his nostrils, but made no effort to attack. We were about the same age, but I was a few inches taller and broader across the shoulders. I dragged him away and shoved him against a tree; my fist cocked back in preparation to punch. "What. Is. Her. Name?" I snarled, scraping rock bottom of my oft-taxed well of patience.

"Alex." The whisper was so soft that even my dragon-enhanced hearing barely caught it. The brown haired boy, who up until now had been keeled over unconscious on his rangy gray dragon, was upright, barely. He was swaying, hugging his chest like he could hold the blood in by force of will alone. "I'm Meisha," he croaked. "That's Orion."

"Why?" the boy named Orion snapped. "Why would you tell them?!"

"They've already shot us!" Meisha shot back with surprising venom; I flinched, even though it wasn't directed toward me. "What else would they do if I didn't?"

Orion bowed his head, suddenly limp in my grip. "You're right," he admitted.

I forced myself to scoff, to take the attention away from the fact that this hadn't been a chance encounter, that we had lain in wait for them. "How touching," I sneered. "Come on."

I pulled a white plastic zip tie from my belt, sliding and tightening it around Orion's wrists before he knew what was happening. I shoved him forward, in the opposite direction of his friend and his dragon. I took pity on the brown haired boy-Meisha- and allowed him to ride on his dragon rather than making him walk. The dragons were pulled along, with the threat of violence toward their riders if there was any funny business. We couldn't threaten the dragons themselves, as it would take more time and equipment than was readily available to injure them any more. We could, however, do anything we liked to the riders. The entire plan hinged upon it.

Orion stumbled as he stepped off the rugged dirt road. I watched, half hoping he'd fall, but he gathered himself and regained his balance. Our enormous livestock trailer, which had been specially modified to haul dragons and riders, sat waiting with open doors. A sleek, ominous black pickup truck was hitched to the shining silver hauler. The dragons went in first, muzzled and shackled, their wounds already cared for. The riders' wounds would be attended later. Perry had pulled Meisha off his dragon. He was now strapped to a gurney, alongside Alex, similarly restrained. I glanced over while waiting for the dragons to settle and caught a flash of Orion's vicious smirk.

"What?" I demanded aggressively. His smirk never wavered; in fact, it broadened.

"She will not take waking up strapped to a stretcher well," he shot back. I sighed inwardly. He was many things, obnoxious and annoying first and foremost, but in this case, he was probably also right. I'd only spoken to her briefly, when she'd already been coping with being shot. What would it be like to speak to her in top form? Something told me it would be, ah, entertaining, at least.

Chapter Seventeen

ALEX

Have you ever had that feeling when you stand up way too fast and the world swims, even though your eyes are closed? That's how I felt when I finally made the long trek back to the land of the living. Or the land of the awake, at least.

Every Saturday of the summer, Coach made the entire hockey team practice for hours. Even with rest, during those times, I felt like there were steel chains wrapped tightly around my chest. That's how it felt now. Needless to say, not a pleasant feeling to wake up to.

Everything came rushing back to me in a tidal wave of memories: being ambushed, being shot, being kidnapped, and the rest of my team. My worry for Meisha spiked, followed quickly by the worry for Orion and Stellar. There had been so much blood. I had no way of knowing if they'd even survived, let alone what kind of shape they'd be in.

I blinked my eyes open slowly, cringing and half-closing them when a bright, irritating light assailed them. "Oh, sorry," a voice said, sounding like a lightbulb had been lit. Something shuffled, and the lights dimmed considerably. "How are you feeling?"

I tried to sit up, and promptly discovered why I felt like something was binding my chest. Because there was. Thick, wide leather bands strapped my upper chest, wrists, and ankles to a standard issue gurney. I was laying on ample padding, pristine white cushions, so I didn't feel cramped or uncomfortable. If not for the straps, it would have been a perfectly acceptable arrangement.

"Where is my team?" I gasped. My struggling against the straps was putting pressure on my bullet wounds, making my head swirl light-headedly. The black-haired boy's worried face swam into view. His large hand pushed my shoulder gently back down.

"Your team is fine," he soothed. I tilted my head, trying to convey my skepticism without words. My muscles throbbed and trembled weakly. "And your dragon," he added, somehow sensing the next question on my long list.

I tried to sit up again. "Why should I believe you?" I pointed out.

"Stop that," he chided. "You'll tear up your stitches. You were shot badly; they're only field stitches. Not exactly hospital-quality."

"I'm so terribly sorry that you had to kidnap and shoot us in the middle of nowhere. It must be so inconvenient for you," I said, my voice laced with terrific sarcasm. I could feel what I presumed to be stitches pulling and shifting painfully.

He pressed his palm to his forehead, bending over. "You're right," he conceded.

"If we're going to have a conversation, you should unstrap me," I hinted.

He shook his head, the corner of his full mouth twitching up in a half smile. "I would if I could," he said sincerely. For some reason, I believed him; it annoyed me to no end. "But I can't." He glanced down suddenly. If I'd been wearing anything other than a plain t-shirt, I'd almost have thought that he was looking at my cleavage. Since my tee covered up anything interesting, I knew that wasn't it. "Now look what you've done," he reproached. "They were finished and now you've started them bleeding again."

"How many?" I croaked.

"Bullet wounds?" he checked.

"No, ears," I said mustering enough energy for some sarcasm.

"Three," he said, shaking his head at my feeble attempt at humor. He touched his collarbone, shoulder, and stomach, showing me where the wounds were located. I nodded mutely and leaned back. Now that everything was sinking in, the adrenaline that had made its home in my veins to keep me conscious had decided to take a leave of absence. My bullet wounds throbbed in time to my heartbeat; my stomach heaved with nausea. I let my head fall onto the cushion, closed my eyes, and fell into the darkness.

A hand settled on my shoulder and shook it lightly. I cracked my eyes open reluctantly, and recoiled from the face until I realized who it was.

"Do you want me to let you up?" he asked. "Do you think you can walk?" I nodded soundlessly. I was sure I could walk; I was not, however, sure that I wouldn't fall over if I tried. He undid the straps deftly, putting his big hand in the crook of my elbow to steady me. My legs wobbled, but held.

The boy pulled away for a second, only long enough to step down to the ground. He turned immediately, offering his hand. If he hadn't shot me, I would have said he was being chivalrous. But he had, so it only annoyed me. I lifted my chin and stepped down. My foot slipped on the metal lip of the trailer and slid out from under me. I fell into his chest.

His arms tightened around me reflexively. I flushed darkly and yanked away. Don't get me wrong: I am not the damsel-in-distress type. I've been playing hockey for years and been in my share of scrapes; only recently I'd learned how to use various weapons, including a knife. Speaking of... stupid, stupid, stupid. I should have checked for my dagger the instant I was loose. It was missing, of course, which didn't surprise me at all. We'd also been trained in hand-to-hand combat, but it was not what you'd call my strong suit. Even in top form, I wasn't great. I was not in top form by any stretch of the imagination, so I'd probably only hurt myself more if I tried.

The boy waved for me to follow him. He led me into a squat building, and we stepped straight into what seemed to be the reception area. Chic leather sofas were arrayed around the room, while drooping ferns in ceramic pots wilted in the corners. The tall desk, which I thought might be made of a concrete wall, was guarded by a gargoyle of a woman with tortoiseshell glasses on a cheap golden chain. Three doors were right in a row. The last door had the insignia of a roaring dragon singed in black into the wood; the boy headed unerringly toward the door with the dragon. We stepped inside; my legs nearly gave out.

I walked toward my team, half-jogging with eagerness to reach them. Orion seemed to be in okay shape; the bullet wound in his shoulder and a magnificent bruise on his cheekbone looked to be the worst of it. *The sun will come out tomorrow*, I thought with grim humor. His dark hair was rumpled; his full lower lip was split and swollen.

Meisha looked even worse. He was unconscious on a gurney like the one I'd been on; his tanned surfer-boy skin was sheet white. Two men in white coats with surgical masks wheeled him away. I tamped down my panic. He needed medical attention, and I couldn't provide it, so we'd have to just let it ride until we figured out what to do.

"Will he be okay?" I asked worriedly. That reminded me: I still didn't know the boy's name. I was instantly vexed. Correct me if I'm wrong, but isn't introducing yourself the first thing you do in a conversation? Not, like, the very last.

"What's your name?" I demanded suddenly. "It's kind of conducive to a good conversation if you actually know who you're speaking with."

He blinked and tilted his head. I guessed he was probably running through our conversation in his mind, trying to remember if he had introduced himself. He frowned.

"I didn't introduce myself?" he said, like he couldn't quite remember.

"Would I have asked if you had?" I pointed out testily. Why did everyone insist on doing this?

His slim face cleared. "Point taken," he conceded. "I'm Cobalt." He held out his hand to shake. His fingers were long and slim, like a player's fingers. The ring finger on his left hand was crooked, like it had been broken repeatedly, and I wondered at it. The was a class ring on his other ring finger, thick and silver with an oval onyx stone set in the center. The only other thing he was wearing that could have been considered jewelry was the set of two dog tags dangling from a chain around his neck.

I glared silently at the hand until he took it back. There was no way I was shaking hands with him. Or touching him.

"Do you know who I am?" I tested. He didn't even bother trying to deny that he knew us.

"Alex," he answered, gesturing after the gurney in the direction Meisha had been taken. "That was Meisha." He frowned wryly. "Troublemaker over there is Orion. Weird birthmark on him, too," he observed.

I grunted noncommittally. It was one thing for me to think that, but someone else did it, and it annoyed me. Cobalt stepped away, motioning for me to follow him. We walked away from the reception area. A group of guards followed us silently, but Cobalt tried to motion them back. They gave him droll stares and continued to walk behind us. He sighed, but let it drop. He pressed his palm onto a scanner, which flashed incandescent blue. The door, which seemed to be a reinforced fire door, slid open with a whoosh of stale air. I stepped in.

I went hot-cold with fury. My mind went blank. It was so quiet up there you could have heard a pin drop. I didn't even hesitate, swinging around and launching my fist at Cobalt's face with all my might. Hand-to-hand combat may not be my specialty, but I'll say one thing for David: he can train someone to throw a pretty good punch.

My fist slammed into his jaw. He hadn't been at all prepared, but he knew enough to roll with the blow; it bespoke previous training. The soldiers waded in while I cocked back for another punch; one clocked me with the butt of his gun, right in a bullet wound. I saw stars and twittering birdies; my ears rang like church at high noon.

"Stop!" Cobalt shouted. It pierced the fog around my mind that he'd probably already said that more than once. Trying to save me, maybe. But who, of the two of us, needed saving?

Chapter Eighteen

"I'm not leaving," I insisted stubbornly. "Not unless you carry me out."

One of the soldiers, a hulking mountain of a man with a grizzled, pockmarked face and a scrubby mustache, cracked his knuckles. The pops rang out, eerily like gunshots. "That could be arranged."

I turned my face away in a clear snub. The soldiers had been all for dragging me out of the room where our dragons were being held in chains; Cobalt had vetoed that idea immediately and vehemently. He had that much power, at least. He had conceded, however, that it would be prudent to remove me to another room and zip tie my wrists together. They itched like fire ants, but there wasn't a snowflake's chance in the Sahara that I was going to ask any of the soldiers to loosen them.

Cobalt had left me, giving the soldiers a clear-cut command and a threat: if one of them touched me, they'd have to deal with Cobalt - after they dealt with me. Sort of a compliment too, I suppose.

I stretched my legs; my knees cracked embarrassingly loudly. The soldiers swung their heads around to look.

"What?" I demanded. They turned back to their card game, set up at a folding table.

The room I was in was small, more of a closet than a room where you held prisoners. The soldiers had plopped me down on a short, too-small wooden chair. I felt like Goldilocks in it, my knees practically up to my chest. The men were as far away from me as they could get in such a small room, which wasn't far. The rickety folding table looked like it would collapse under the weight of the deck of cards and the pile of money they were betting.

I'd been trying to reach Stellar intermittently since we'd walked into the building, but no luck. I didn't know why; maybe because of the bullet wounds. I was becoming ever more fed up and frustrated with this whole situation, so I leaned back and closed my eyes.

I must have dozed off, because when I woke up again, Cobalt was walking into the room. A man walked stiffly behind him with an almost military bearing. He wore olive green cargo pants and a beige tee shirt; a gun was strapped to his hip.

I sat up straight. Now it was going to get interesting. The man was practically goose-stepping, swinging his long arms forcefully. He looked like a gorilla, in my humble opinion. The man turned to Cobalt, who was rigid and drawn up to his full height.

"Didn't you have our prisoner's wounds taken care of?" he chided. Not at all how I'd thought he'd sound. I'd expected him to blustering and gruff, not speak to Cobalt like a naughty grandchild. Bit of a letdown.

"I did, sir," he said stiffly. "I believe she must have ripped her stitches when she punched me." I may have been imagining it, but to me that sounded like a subtle reminder that there was a reason I was tied up. I was also slightly vexed that no one who had recently entered my life seemed to be able to introduce themselves; I decided to shorten military man to MM.

I was quite proud of myself. Yes, maybe I'd gotten nailed right in the stitches in the process of being dragged off Cobalt, but I'd managed to make the one shot I had count. The whole left side of his face was swelling; the beginnings of what promised to be a beastly shiner already forming. *You bruise my team, I bruise you,* I thought with grim satisfaction.

"Ah," MM said delicately. "Well, we'll get that taken care of. If you behave yourself, I'll even allow you to see your dragon afterward," he hinted, turning slightly to address me. Bribes don't work if it's what should have been done in the first place.

"Let's do this, then," I said casually. I stood, struggling to keep my footing. Balance with bound hands is an unsure thing at best and a treacherous one at worst.

"Come with me," Cobalt ordered stiffly. He grabbed my arm, just above my elbow, and dragged me along with him. As was my habit when people told me what to do, I dug in my heels and refused to move. "Please," he breathed.

Satisfied and curious, I walked quietly at his side, taking note of where he was leading me. Out of the broom closet, he led me down a long hallway, ugly off-white walls giving the appearance of a small town hospital. Two soldiers peeled themselves reluctantly away from their card game and followed us. Cobalt turned to them.

"I can handle her from here," he said. "You are dismissed."

"Like you handled her earlier?" one said snidely, folding his arms over his chest. The other threw him a glare, obviously set to head back to the card game.

"I doubt your boss will be happy that you disobeyed a direct order," I observed, playing a hunch. "Perhaps you'd like to tell him why?" I continued, falsely polite.

They grumbled, but did an about-face headed back to their lucrative card game, one with an almost comical spring in his step.

When I turned back to Cobalt, he was studying me, face inscrutable. "What?" I demanded again; he shook his head slowly.

"Nothing."

Famous last words.

Chapter Nineteen

"If you don't sit down, I'll sedate you," the woman threatened, clearly at the end of her rope. I hesitated, long enough to decide that she probably meant it, and plopped back down on the crackling paper of the exam room table. Cobalt stood in the corner of the room, back turned. I could see his smug half-grin in the floor-length mirror on the door.

I sidled sideways, making absolutely sure that he couldn't see me in the mirror. The doctor gave me a dry look. I sat on the exam table in my uniform bottoms and a sports bra. My bloodstained gray t-shirt was wadded up in the corner, along with a pile of bloody bandages she'd had to peel away from my skin due to the crusted, rust-red blood from my wounds.

I'd ripped out the majority of my stitches when I'd punched Cobalt, so I had to sit through them being painstakingly removed and carefully put back in. I'd stubbornly refused to let the doctor inject me with anything, even something she claimed was anesthetic, so I had to suffer through it. I'd managed so far, with only the occasional wince.

The lady doctor bent over my stitches, brow furrowed in concentration. She had a sort of bleached complexion, like she'd once been tan but spent too much time inside to maintain it. Her dirty blond hair was pulled back in a severe bun. She had functional, rectangular black glasses that sat high on her nose. Her white lab coat was buttoned tightly to her throat. The tag clipped to it was turned around, probably an attempt to prevent me from reading it. Bit of a wasted effort, since I could see through it when she turned toward the light. Avaline Marks. Pretty name.

Even through the haze of pain, I still worried for my team. I'd seen the dragons, so I knew they were somewhat alright, if in poor conditions. What I didn't know was Meisha's condition or what they'd done with Orion. Cobalt claimed he'd punched one too many soldiers and they'd locked him up. I was kind of proud of him, in fact.

"Done," the doctor sighed, standing back to look over her work with a critical eye.

I glanced down, too. Having seen my fair amount of stitches, most of them in my own body, I knew the tiny, neat striations were better than most could have managed. Better than I could have, anyway. She was a professional. I shuddered to think how many stitches she'd put in before, and would after.

The skin around my abs was pinched and puckered; the black thread used for the stitches stood out starkly against my almost luminescent skin. The shoulder wasn't as bad, probably because that bullet hadn't been as deeply embedded.

While I'd been studying my new stitches, Cobalt had wandered over to do the same. I froze, suddenly painfully aware that I wasn't wearing a shirt. Goosebumps rippled along my skin, raising the pale hair.

"It could have been worse," Cobalt said, sounding relieved. I bit back a smart aleck remark about who had shot me and stood, hoping the doctor would get the hint. She did.

"You need to keep those covered up," she instructed, her tone businesslike. "You'll have to come back in every day for me to change them." As she spoke, she dug around in the only cupboard without a lock, coming up with a plain-Jane beige t-shirt. She tossed it to me; I moved to catch it without thinking. My stitches screamed in protest; I sucked air tightly between my teeth, producing a satisfying whistling sound like a cannonball being dropped. Cobalt glanced at me, concerned. I waved him off and struggled grimly into the shirt, taking it slow.

A cell phone warbled. Cobalt fished in one of his cargo pockets and came out with an outdated flip phone. His blue eyes slid back and forth as he scanned the glowing screen.

"Come on," he said, holding his hand out to help me off the table. It had a scar I hadn't noticed before, a raised rope of ghost white bisecting his palm from the base of his pointer finger to the opposite heel of his hand. "We're going to see your dragon. Your boy will be there too."

I couldn't help the noise that slipped out of my mouth. It sounded like a pig squeal, only even higher pitched. I hadn't been aware, until that moment, that my voice was even capable of reaching that pitch. Normally, I would have been mortified, but right now I didn't even care. I leapt off the table, ignoring my stitches' screeching protests as I jounced them. "Let's go."

Chapter Twenty

I flew across the room. Cobalt twisted out of the way as I flew past him, crooning to Stellar both physically and mentally. She was muzzled and chained, and the chains ran through a sturdy ring set deep into the stone floor. She bent her head over my shoulder, the best she could do while so restricted. I ran my hand down her side, and when I reached her wing, she flinched,

I stepped back, studying her with the same critical eye I had applied to my stitches. Even carefully cleaned and cared for, her left wing was shredded. Flaps of webbing and skin had been pulled together in an attempt to accelerate the healing process, but I doubted it would help much.

It hurts, she confided softly. I twitched, completely unprepared for the first mental contact I'd had since we got here. Wherever here was. *I know*, I soothed.

The door hissed open. Orion stumbled in, having been shoved from behind by a very fed-up-looking guard. His hand kept twitching toward his gun; I sympathized. If Orion really wanted to annoy you, he really would.

His stumble ran him into my chest. I threw my arms out reflexively to catch him; we ended up in a very unorthodox hugging position. His hands were bound behind him, so he lowered his head over my shoulder in a move eerily similar to the one Stellar had finished just moments before. His sigh ruffled my hair, which was falling out of my hurried ponytail. His chest rumbled against mine; it took me a second to realize he was speaking, in a voice too quiet for anyone else to hear.

"I was worried about you," he whispered fervently. "I'm so glad you're okay." He stepped back, studying me critically. "You are okay, aren't you?" he checked.

I made a so-so motion with my hand, tilting it back and forth like a ship at sea. "Mostly okay."

Cobalt piped up from behind us, his voice dark and deathly quiet. "Three bullet wounds and eighteen stitches."

"Whose fault is that?" Orion snarled with surprising rancor. Cobalt was unfazed.

"The situation got out of hand," he admitted stiffly.

"You bet it did." Orion sneered.

The soldier who'd shoved Orion stepped forward, raising his meaty fist. "I've had about enough of you."

Stellar rumbled darkly behind me, her chest vibrating with the sound. *The same could be said for you, big boy.*

I held up my hands, making a time-out T. "Everybody, chill," I ordered. Surprisingly, they listened.

Stellar raised her head suddenly, nostrils flaring. The ridges above them crinkled as she sniffed, pulling in big gulps of air to fill her vast lungs. A huge shadow approached at Cobalt's back. He lifted his hand and held it out backwards, the way only someone who knew exactly who was there and what they were could do.

The dragon licked the hand and continued forward, bumping his head affectionately against Cobalt's shoulder; he stumbled forward a step, but balanced with the ease of long practice. A messenger dragon strode forward, his webbed wings rustling. The dragon was jade green, which lightened to emerald on his belly. His eyes were the mossy green of filtered forest light; his head was large and noble, with a strong nose and square jaw. Quite similar to Cobalt, in fact, though Cobalt's jaw was sharper. Maybe his rider?

The dragon lifted his great head and stared down at me. *You hit my rider?*

I nodded slowly. "I did," I agreed warily. I wasn't entirely sure who he was referring to, considering that I'd hit multiple people today, but a dragon always knows when their rider is hurt. He probably knew who hit his rider the second after I did it.

The dragon huffed and bobbed his head once. *It was a good hit,* he approved. Cobalt made a face at him. Ah, that answered that question.

"My dragon, Steel," Cobalt said wryly. I lifted my hand and waved gently, then flushed beet red. Cobalt grinned at my embarrassment; I glared.

I bent my knees and settled myself next to Cobalt, leaning back against the wall to watch the reunion. Cobalt had finally convinced the guards to untie Orion; he hugged Tyne like he'd never let him go. Tyne had his muzzle on Orion's shoulder, standing as close as they could get, practically on top of each other. They didn't seem to mind.

"So what now?" I asked quietly.

Cobalt glanced over. "I'll explain some things. After I'm finished, we'll move you guys to a barn, which is where you'll be staying until the bosses decide what to do with you."

"Okay," I said agreeably. "But I want to see Meisha before I go anywhere."

He frowned. "I don't know."

I pointed at Maath, who stood in the corner dejectedly, his muzzle brushing the floor. He'd made no attempt to greet me when I'd walked in, which worried me. Usually, he was as friendly as a dog, greeting anyone he knew happily and wholeheartedly. With his rider gone, he wasn't feeling it. I was as worried about Meisha as Maath was, but a sad dragon could turn into an angry dragon in the blink of an eye. Of the two, you wanted the latter the least.

I flipped my hand. "Start explaining."

Chapter Twenty-One

C obalt's explanation was a doozy. If I believed him, that is, which I wasn't entirely sure about. This place was called The Base. It was a military installment, similar to Project Rediscovery. The wild dragon from the story Hale had told me, back at Rediscovery? It had chosen a rider after hatching, the first known and possibly only one to do so. The young dragon and its rider had fled from the scientists, fearing for their lives.

They had begun to steal eggs from the scientists, one by one. Like the Robin Hood of dragons, except they didn't give the wealth away. They had taken the eggs and searched out riders for each, creating a sort of anti-Rediscovery. All these years, The Base had quietly sabotaged Project Rediscovery at every opportunity.

"How many other riders have you kidnapped?" I asked, trying to sound casual. I picked at the dirt and blood beneath my fingernails, trying to seem as if the answer to this question didn't concern me, when it very much did.

Cobalt hesitated.

"How many?" I snapped, just a few decibels below a yell. Orion twisted around, wide-eyed and worried. I waved him off. He turned slowly back to Tyne, who dropped his head again.

That shook him out of his stupor. "None!" he shouted back. We fumed in silence until I got up and walked over to Orion. We talked quietly, but with no way to stop the guards from listening in, we couldn't talk about anything of importance. Like, say, escape, for example.

It took Cobalt fifteen minutes to cool down. He paced the room, muttering mutinously under his breath, throwing the occasional glare at Orion and me. We leaned against our dragons, crouched uncomfortably due to the chains and muzzles. Stellar was actually asleep, the back of her head shoved up against my back at an angle. I, personally, didn't know how she could sleep in that position; to each her own, I suppose.

"Come on," Cobalt said grumpily. I put my hand on the floor to stand, offering it to Orion once I was standing. "No," Cobalt said sharply. "Her, only."

I glanced at him, determined he was serious, and nodded slowly. "Stay here," I told Orion. "And don't make any trouble."

He stuck his tongue out halfheartedly, as though I'd ruined his fun.

"I mean it," I warned. He sobered, and nodded seriously. I could see him readying to turn back to Tyne. I didn't have to worry. I knew they wouldn't move an inch from one another anytime soon. "Good."

I'll be back, I told Stellar. I doubt it even penetrated her deep sleep, but I wouldn't have felt right if I didn't at least try to tell her.

I turned back to Cobalt. "Lead on."

Chapter Twenty-Two

"I want to go in," I insisted.

"No," the nurse insisted right back.

I glared and crossed my arms over my chest, glaring down from the heights at the young woman. She was probably at least ten years older than me, but I was a good six inches taller. Blessed with height, I guess.

She wasn't cowed. "You can't go in there. He's resting."

"I need to see him!"

"Miss? Are you Alex?"

I turned. "Why?"

The woman's pretty face drooped in relief. "You are. Cobalt's on his way back." Finished with delivering her message, she waved slightly and scurried away before I could get a word out. I stared after her. The nurse I'd been arguing with had taken advantage of my distraction; she'd vanished.

I tried the door handle, although I knew it would be locked. I plopped down across the hall, staring stubbornly at the nondescript door. I guessed it was late; the few windows I could see from my unique vantage point looked dark. I could even see a few stars. Nurses and doctors bustled around, stepping through open doors to check on their patients. There wasn't as much staff as a typical hospital would have;

they probably didn't need it if they only had a certain amount of riders they needed to care for. All the other doors that I could see were wide open, inviting people in.

The walls were an ugly shade of ecru, seeming to stretch in all directions. The same painting in the same square frame was spaced along the wall at intervals. I stared at the swirls of dark blue and violet, lilac and green. I assumed it was a flower. It could just as easily been a boat or... I tilted my head. Anything, really.

Boot heels clicked on the checkered gray tiles. Cobalt approached, wearing what I assumed must be his uniform. The fitted leather riding jacket was open, revealing the fleece lining. His undershirt was ebony black, with a stripe of lime green slashing across his chest from left shoulder to right hip. His pants weren't cargos like mine; they seemed to be soft black jeans, not as fitted as skinny jeans. His boots were black like mine, and the dog tags I'd seen earlier glinted at his long throat.

He stopped, standing above me. I tilted my head back. Even standing, I had to look up a little, but on the floor, it was a long way up.

"I hear you've been causing trouble," he said. His voice was disapproving, but the corner of his full mouth tilted up at the corners.

"I have," I agreed pleasantly. No need to deny it. "They won't let me in to see Meisha."

He frowned contemplatively. "I'll see what I can do. But," he continued, seeing an ear-to-ear grin spread across my face. "It won't be until tomorrow, at the earliest. You should get some sleep."

"I'm not leaving," I insisted. "I'll sit here all night if I have to."

"I could make you," he pointed out.

My grin morphed to a smug smirk. "You could try," I said sweetly.

"Please?" he pleaded. "I'll try to get you in tomorrow, but it would be better if you guys and your dragons slept in the dragon barn tonight."

I sighed and considered. I was exhausted, and there was little to be gained from sitting here all night, other than proving how stubborn I was, and Cobalt had probably figured that out already. "Fine."

Cobalt

When I arrived at the barn in the middle of the night to check on Alex, I expected her and Orion to be waiting at the door, teeth chattering, wanting to come inside. It would serve them both right for being a pain. The dragon barn was kept cold at all times; it helped the dragons sleep.

Instead, they didn't seem to be there at all. I poked my head into the stalls, one by one, to see if they'd commandeered it to sleep in. The stalls were like horse stalls, only bigger. The top part of each was barred; the bottom, which would typically have been wood, was made of metal. The designers of our dragon barns had done their best to stay away from flammable materials, for obvious reasons. There were only seven stalls in the barn, along with the stall that had been converted into a tack room. Each rider had a saddle and saddlebags. I was fascinated at the differences between our saddles and Alex's. Hers was of much better quality. I wondered who had made it.

Alex's dragon- what was it called? Stellar- houghed a warning from the third stall on my right. The door of the stalls the dragons slept in was open. Why hadn't I noticed right way? To my shock, Alex popped her head out from under Stellar's wing, yawning.

"What's up?" she mumbled sleepily, rubbing her eyes with one hand.

I opened my mouth to speak, but sputtered to a stop when Orion popped up too.

"What?" he asked grumpily. Alex waved her hand loosely at him.

"Go back to bed. I've got this." I arched my brows at what that sounded like, but let it slide. I was pretty sure they weren't... not that it mattered if they were. It wasn't really any of my business either way.

"Just checking on you guys," I said nonchalantly, shrugging casually.

Alex gave me a knowing look; she clearly wasn't fooled. "You thought we'd be begging to come inside," she grinned. I grunted noncommittally. Was I really that easy to read? I studied her silently. How could she sleep like that? More to the point, how did her dragon let her sleep like that? I couldn't imagine the trust necessary to do something like that. The rider would have to trust that the dragon wouldn't roll on them, wouldn't suffocate under their wing… the possibilities were endless, on both sides.

"What?" she demanded, clearly out of patience. I shook myself and blushed.

"Just thinking," I admitted. "Steel would never let me-" I waved my hand to encompass her, under her dragon's wing. "Let me do that."

"How do you know?" she reasoned.

I hadn't really thought about it like that. "I don't," I decided finally.

"Great. Now that we've figured that out, go away." She made shooing motions with her hands, yawning again. I grinned inwardly.

"Good night," I murmured. She snuggled under Stellar's wing and promptly fell asleep.

Orion

The Base rider who woke me up this morning nearly gave me a heart attack. I had finally gotten back to sleep, after a long, cold night. Cobalt, one of the other riders, had stopped by in the middle of the night. I suspected, and it was confirmed by his conversation with Alex, that he was trying to freeze us out. The barn was chilly, but underneath Tyne's wing, I was warm and cozy. I'd popped up in the middle of their conversation, trying to give her an excuse to kick him to the curb, but she hadn't taken it. It made me angry and jealous; also, curious. Why wouldn't she send him away? It was the middle of the night; there was obviously a sketchy reason for him being there. Duh! But I digress. If she wanted to be stupid, that was her prerogative.

The Base rider kicked me awake this morning, literally. By the time I got my eyes open and figured out what the heck was going on, he had his foot drawn back to kick Alex. I waited with bated breath; no one reacts well to being kicked awake. When that kick produced no results, he pulled back to kick her again, his malicious grin betraying his intention to hit her even harder. I slithered out from under Tyne's wing, shoving my foot in the path of his strike. He glared. I glared back.

"I'll wake her," I said softly, ending our silent standoff. He made a rude gesture and stalked off with his nose in the air.

Stellar lifted her head. So did Alex, peering out from under her wing, perfectly awake and composed. "I'm awake."

I offered my hand awkwardly, not sure how much she'd heard. She took it, tightening her long fingers around mine and flexing her knees to stand. "Cobalt sent a rider to wake us up early. He didn't say why," I said, not bothering to hide my annoyance.

I glanced up when a new shadow formed on the ground. Just in time to see Cobalt stride in, looking like the cat that hijacked the milk truck.

"Speak of the devil, and he shall appear," I said coolly. Cobalt glared at me, then shifted his attention to Alex like I didn't even exist.

"You need to stay here. I'm working on getting you access to Meisha, but I'll be gone for a while," he said quietly, speaking to everyone but me. "You'll get in trouble if you leave, and I don't want to have to deal with that."

I snickered viciously and pounced on the remark. "We'll 'get in trouble'," I sneered, practically breathless with spiteful laughter. I made air quotes around the words, making it as sarcastic as I was capable of. "Do we look like some shy little kid who won't make eye contact or talk back to teachers? We've all been in trouble before; I'm sure we will be again. Possibly soon," I added.

Cobalt opened his mouth, looking ready to tear into me. Alex spoke, stopping him cold in his tracks.

Chapter Twenty-Three

ALEX

"That's enough," I said firmly, fed up with their bickering. "Cobalt, I may not agree with everything he's saying, but I am deeply, deeply unimpressed that you're sticking us in the barn." Cobalt looked hurt and surprised, but Orion looked smug. I wasn't finished. "Orion, Cobalt has been better to us than anyone else in this venture. You might want to consider treating him well so that he continues to do so. At the very least be civil."

Orion's smug grin dropped off his face, and it took another place on Cobalt's.

"Do what you can," I told Cobalt. "We'll entertain ourselves." He looked nervous. I could almost see the gears turning sluggishly under his mop of thick black hair. I could also see the precise moment when the gears stopped and he made the conscious decision to put aside any misgivings he may have had and trust us.

"It's not my choice," he said, his voice pleading. "But I'll be punished if you don't."

Orion barked a laugh. "Is that supposed to convince us?" I elbowed him in the side, but I half-agreed. If he was trying to guilt us, he was barking up the wrong tree with Orion, who clearly hated the Base rider with a passion. I didn't blame him. Actually, I wasn't sure why I didn't hate him. I didn't know, and I wasn't inclined to find out.

I took another step, staring at the ground, and nearly ran into something. Or rather, someone. My nose was level with the hollow at the base of someone's throat.

"Hello," a husky, familiar voice said. I jerked my head up, nearly smacking him in the chin. Meisha looked pale and wan, but relatively steady on his feet. I stepped back so I could see his face rather than his chest, not that that was a bad view either.

"What are you doing out of the mini-hospital?" I asked suspiciously. When they'd refused to let me see him, they had made it seem like he was on his deathbed. Here he was, standing and seemingly healthy. Or, at least, not like he was going to keel over and die within the next five minutes.

"They let me out," he shrugged, which seemed a wee bit obvious to me.

Just as obviously, the shrug was a bad idea. His face drained of color and he swayed on his feet; I lunged to catch him as he tipped backward. I placed my fingers on his neck, feeling for a pulse; there, but thready and weak.

I reached frantically for Stellar; even though I knew she was only a few hundred feet away in the barn, it felt like we were separated by a vast ocean. As she was when she was bored, Stellar slept deeply. I rallied my mental strength and did the mind-speaking equivalent of shouting into her ear. *Get Steel to bring Cobalt here now.*

Dragons could mind-speak with any dragon or human, more easily and reliably than even their riders. It was simpler to create a chain through our dragons than to attempt to send it ourselves.

He's on his way, she sent tersely.

Cobalt stalked in two minutes later, clearly on the warpath. I refused to let him get a word in edgewise. "Meisha just collapsed," I informed him. "What are we going to do?"

His long lashed eyes closed for a second. He was either praying for patience or thinking about what to do, I wasn't sure which. Maybe both.

"Medics are on their way," he reported. "We aren't supposed to touch him until they arrive." I could do that. Let the professionals do what they should have done before they released him from the hospital.

Chapter Twenty-Four

"I did not release him," the doctor fumed.

I favored him with a dry look. "Thank you. I figured that out when he fainted."

Meisha spoke up from the next room. "No, I didn't!"

"Yes, you did!" I yelled back.

"Maybe we should conduct this conversation elsewhere," a nurse suggested delicately.

"Is he going to be okay?" a voice behind me said. I whirled. Cobalt shifted back a step.

"I think so," I said with a frown. "They won't tell me anything else. If they don't let me see him, I'll go outside and climb up to his window," I warned.

"Like a spider?" To his credit, Cobalt kept the sarcasm out of his voice.

I nodded solemnly, trying to fight back my grin. "Exactly." To my shock, Cobalt put his hands on my arms and rubbed up and down gently. I stepped forward into his arms and hugged his chest. He stiffened, then returned the gesture.

Whatever he and anyone else thought, I was not the kind of the girl who needed hugs often. I had a strong suspicion that... yes! My dagger was tugged into the waistband of his jeans. I hugged him tighter, reached down and... he skipped back.

"Sneaky," he grinned, wagging a finger at me. "But not sneaky enough."

I shrugged. "A girl's gotta try," I said innocently, holding my hands out to the sides, palms up. He shook his head, a slow smile on his lips. Thwarted, I plopped down on the ground and leaned against the wall, shivering at the chill of the whiteness. Cobalt sank down beside me.

"I'm not going to fight with you about leaving," he said softly. "I understand the instinct to protect your men." He sounded sad, almost introspective; I glanced at him out of the side of my eye. He face was gloomy, brooding.

I was stunned. I'd nearly forgotten that he was a leader too, and probably in a far larger capacity than I was. My future job was to be a leader, but not the kind that led a team. I was to speak for all of us, which was far scarier to me. It made me question how much he'd lost, dragon and human alike. It also made my stomach clench to think that I might sound like that one day, so miserable and self-loathing. Especially if I continued on the path I walked now.

Even if we escaped from the Base, we were going back to the same thing with Project Rediscovery. Yes, they'd been kind to us so far, but they weren't all that different from the people holding us captive now. It was just a different sort of captivity, one of chains and walls, one of words and secrets. I saw no way out, no way to escape all these people who sought to use Stellar and me for their own purposes. I wasn't even sure there was an escape, only learning to deal with it over time.

After a few minutes, my shock and pain started to set in. My eyelids fluttered, but I couldn't keep them open. Finally I gave up, leaned my head back against the wall, and dropped into sleep.

Cobalt

I nearly jumped out of my boots when Alex's head thudded onto my shoulder. She'd punched me in the face, which, by the way, had hurt, and now she was- I cracked my eyes open slowly and torqued my body slightly to study her, careful not to disturb her.

Pale eyelids sheathed clear green eyes, gold-ringed and wide-pupiled. Lengthy, curving black lashes with tawny roots brushed high cheekbones.

She'd fallen asleep again. How long had she slept over the past few days?

A lock of silky brown hair swept across her face. My hand moved of its own volition, tucking it back her ear. She didn't even twitch, nor did her deep, even breathing change.

A nurse stepped out of Meisha's room, opening her mouth to report. I gestured frantically for her to shut up, and she looked relieved.

The nurse crouched, whispering in my ear that Meisha was going to be okay. He'd pushed himself too hard and passed out. She glanced down at Alex.

"I'm a little worried about her, though," she murmured. "She sleeps too much."

I raised my eyebrows, like *and?*

"We'll check her out later, after she wakes up."

I couldn't help let out a groan. She'd be ecstatic about that. The nurse grinned vindictively at my expression. I glared. "We'll take care of it," she promised.

I snorted as she walked away. Luck to them, then. I settled myself more comfortably, careful not to jostle Alex. If she wanted to use me for a pillow, fine. I wasn't moving until she did.

Chapter Twenty-Five

"Get up!" I shot to awareness, reflexively going for my dagger, which was gone. The empty sheath hung there; it wouldn't do much good.

Cobalt must have had the same thought, as he went first for his own knife, then his back to check that I hadn't stolen my knife back while we slept. I wished I had, but no such luck.

The nurse spoke, and I brought my attention back to her reluctantly. "Meisha's fine," she promised. "But we want to check you out."

I balked. "I'm fine."

The nurse wasn't buying it. "You were shot."

"I'm really, really okay," I tried.

Cobalt startled me by wrapping an arm around me and leaning closer, nuzzling his face against my shoulder. "Bargain for it," he breathed. "Tell them you'll get checked out if they let you see Meisha."

I decided that was an excellent idea; Stellar agreed. I passed it on, and the nurse agreed immediately, obviously relieved. She, and most likely anyone else who had met me, were probably of the same opinion: it was easier to make a deal with the devil than fight with me. The lesser of two evils.

She swiped her card to unlock the door and stepped aside.

I peeked around the depressingly-gray door. Meisha brightened instantly when he saw me. He was Casper-the-friendly-ghost white, and hooked up to enough machinery to run the world. He patted the bed next to him; I settled where he'd indicated, my bullet wounds screaming obscenities. His black ringed, bluish-purple eyes studied me in concern. I waved him off.

"I'm fine." He arched an eyebrow at me, but didn't call me on it.

"They're not going to let me out," he complained. I laughed.

"Drama queen," I chided. "They have to let you out eventually."

Meisha sobered. "Do they?" he asked quietly. His voice begged for an answer, for reassurance that I couldn't give him. I didn't have an answer, so I leaned back against the plastic headboard, resting shoulder-to-shoulder with Meisha. I told him about the doppelganger photos in the hallway, how it was the same painting all the way down. He shared his nasty hospital food with me when they brought him lunch.

Cobalt cleared his throat. Out of respect for our, or possibly my, privacy, he'd waited in the hallway for the hour and a half I'd been in Meisha's room. "Alex, it's time to leave," he said quietly. He sounded regretful, like he was sorry I had to leave. I believed it; he hadn't had any objections to me visiting my teammate to begin with. "It's time for your checkup."

I huffed, but didn't really feel the inclination to pick another fight just yet.

"That's cold!" I blurted indignantly. The freezing head of the stethoscope was pressed against the pale skin of my ribcage, then lower back. The doctor squinted in concentration, then frowned.

"Something is wrong," he announced. I resisted the urge to point out the obvious, *Duh, I was shot,* but managed to hold my tongue. "Your heart is too slow."

I debated whether or not to tell him. It would probably bring on another round of tests and questions. "It's not too slow."

The doctor looked puzzled; it quickly transitioned to anger.

"Yes, it is," he insisted.

I corrected myself. "It's not too slow for me," I explained. "We're mentally-and physically- linked to giant lizards. It changes our bodies, including slowing down our heart rates."

We sat in one of the exam rooms. A stretcher had been hurriedly brought into the room; they wanted us both in the room so they could ask questions. If one of us didn't know, the other might. Meisha had felt left out; he wasn't missing much.

Orion and I both sat without our shirts, which was freezing cold. Goosebumps rippled along my pale skin. Even though I felt like an Alexsicle, I could still appreciate the view of Orion without a shirt. His abs weren't just a six pack; eight pack, at least, so ripped you could have grated cheese on them. He had broad shoulders with well-defined biceps, tapering to trim hips. It was much the same with me, but it's one thing to see it on yourself; it's quite another to see it on a boy who wasn't exactly unattractive to begin with.

The doctor still didn't believe me about our heart rates, so I challenged him to try it on the other riders. It wouldn't work on Meisha, obviously, but it would on Orion.

He shuddered when the stethoscope touched his bare chest. The doctor frowned. I just sat there with a smug grin on my face; I was right, he just needed time to figure it out.

"Why is it like that?" he demanded. Orion and I shrugged in unison.

"Why does your heart beat like it does?" I pointed out, a little bit indignant. I couldn't explain why my heart was the way it was. Cobalt mouthed that the doctor was new, which explained quite a bit.

The doctor was miffed at being proven wrong, but he recovered long enough to say that he would like to run some more tests. I just nodded and smiled. There was no way. He was lucky that I'd gotten checked out to begin with.

Cobalt marched us back to the stables. I was angry again because they hadn't let Orion and me in to say goodbye to Meisha.

As Cobalt turned around, I called after him. "We'd like to start eating with you," I said.

He looked puzzled and wary. "Why?" he asked suspiciously.

I frowned, not sure how to phrase it. Best to go with the simple approach. "We aren't getting enough food," I admitted. "We need like six thousand calories a day and we aren't getting it." He blinked, then face-palmed. I blinked too.

"I'm so sorry," he said fervently. "I should have known that you guys would have the same dietary needs that we do. I'll take care of it."

"Bye."

Chapter Twenty-Six

I t wasn't the first time I'd felt like this, but I wasn't anxious for it to happen again.

I felt like a zoo animal. Meisha had been released from the hospital on a probationary basis. Cobalt had arranged for us to eat in the main hall with the Base riders. The hall had fallen completely silent as soon as we'd stepped in.

Cobalt didn't seem to notice. However, my team and I were uncomfortably aware. I took the opportunity to study the other riders.

Unlike us, Base riders all wore the same uniform, except for who I assumed to be the leaders. Their uniform was just like Cobalt's, with the only variances being the colors.

I also noticed another difference: hair color. Unlike at Project Rediscovery, where you were free to have piercings or dyed hair if you chose, I saw none of that here. A sea of brown, black, and blond hair spilled across the hall; a few redheads popped up here and there like red daisies in a hay field. No blue, pink, or purple highlights.

The hall was a mass of long trestle tables crammed with food. Platters of bacon, sausage, and pancakes. Bowls of eggs, applesauce, and grits. Pitchers of orange juice, insulated ones I assumed were coffee, and milk, with all the fixings you needed. The food was the same up and down the table, with multiples of each dish.

Cobalt led us to the back of the room, to a smaller table tucked into a shadowy nook. Five people already sat there, but Cobalt took no notice.

Three boys and two girls held court at the small table. The girl nearest to me was the stereotypical California girl. Corn silk blonde hair, icy blue eyes, and clear, tanned skin with no tan lines. Her uniform was almost too tight, accentuating her... shall we call them assets? It was white and bright pink, something I wouldn't have gone near with a fireman's ladder. Whereas my pants were just that, pants, the bottom of her uniform flared out into a skirt, with leggings beneath. She was thin and curvy, with full pink lips and a straight, pert nose. She glared at me immediately; I glared back.

The other girl sat on her right side. She was Asian, with slanted brown eyes and angular features. Her black hair cascaded like a waterfall over her slender shoulders, flowing down her back. She was thin and small. The uniform she wore was smoky gray and lavender, hugging her curves. It was oriental style, tight and silky, with a slit up the side so she could move. Her shirt had a slit too, revealing a few inches of her side. Her riding jacket was tossed over the back of her chair, as were the others'.

One of the boys scooted over to make room for us. He had brown hair, long in the front and swept to the side, shorter in the back. His eyes were bright, lively green, set beneath dark eyebrows. His uniform was more of a tunic, a baggy hunter green top that tapered toward his hips. The bottom was black jeans, with vines embroidered from thigh to knee. He had a dagger sheath on his hip, unlike most. The hilt had the same vine designs all the way down into the sheath. The boy smiled and gave us a friendly grin, not at all put out by the fact that everyone else was glaring at us...

...Including another of the boys. He had sandy blond hair and blue eyes, with freckles on the bridge of his nose and cheekbones. He looked like a surfer. His uniform top was fitted like a surf top, and the bottoms were really long board shorts. The boy scooted too, to make sure there wasn't enough room for us.

The last at the table looked like Cobalt. The same black hair and devastating blue eyes, roughly the same features. It looked like someone had taken features and streamlined them for Cobalt, leaving the original for this boy. His shoulders were broader, straining his fox-red top. He had cargos like me in a dusty gray. His face didn't change when he saw us, but he did throw an exasperated glance at Cobalt, who pointedly ignored him.

"Scoot over," Cobalt ordered. Surfer-boy slid reluctantly. I sat down next to Cobalt, leaving Meisha and Orion sandwiched between the girls. They didn't seem to mind. In fact, I was pretty sure Orion and the Asian girl slid closer together.

"Dig in," the green eyed boy said happily. "I'm Aimery," he continued, extending his hand. I shook it; he offered it to the boys without hesitation.

"You needn't be so happy all the time, Aim," Surfer-boy said grumpily.

"And why not?" Aimery demanded.

"It's unnatural," Surfer-boy said slyly, making sure to look straight at me as he spoke.

I glared back as I reached for a plate, heaping food onto it. Sausage, bacon, eggs, and a biscuit made a sandwich. I poured orange juice as I ate, chewing in ecstasy.

A window-shaking roar echoed through the hall. Everyone jumped and looked around. I bit my lip to keep from giggling, then gave up and burst out laughing.

"What?" Aimery asked, glancing between Cobalt and me, like Cobalt could explain.

"My dragon is very much enjoying her meal," I gasped, breathless with laughter. Two identical roars shook the room; Orion and Meisha joined in my laughter. So did Aimery, with clear, pure laughter.

Cobalt cleared his throat. "Clearly introductions are in order," he said reproachfully, giving the other riders the stink eye. He pointed them out one by one. "This is Scipio. Skip for short." That was surfer boy, who clearly didn't like me. I didn't particularly like him either. He glared, like he was daring me to comment on his name. I wouldn't have given him the satisfaction even if I'd had something to say. "Ice," Cobalt continued, pointing out the blond girl, who was united with Skip in her dislike of me. Aptly named, as her blue eyes were frosty as snowflakes straight from the cloud. "Tiara," was the Asian girl; she gave me a friendly smile and dipped her head in recognition.

Cobalt sighed, clearly not relishing introducing the next. "And my brother, Micah," he mumbled, staring off to the side. I took another bite, unsure how to respond to that, or even if a response was warranted.

"Ashamed of me, little brother?" Micah asked, leaning forward like a cat about to pounce. I shifted too, unsure of what was going on between them.

"No," Cobalt said tightly.

"The food's good," I interrupted, glaring at Micah, a silent warning to back off. He leaned back and folded his arms, the picture of casual breakfast conversation.

"The cooks are very good at what they do," Aimery said, eager to please.

"I'd hate to wash dishes around here," I mused, more to myself than anyone.

Ice sneered, obviously having overheard my near-silent observation. "You do your own dishes?" she scoffed. It's amazing how someone so short managed to look down her short nose at me, but Ice managed.

"Yes," I said sweetly. "My parents are prominent doctors. They don't really have time for dishes." If she wanted to be all high-and-mighty, I could play that card too.

"Oh," she managed flatly.

I continued eating, slathering syrup onto fluffy pancakes and chopping them up with my fork. For the first time since we'd been brought to The Base, we actually had real silverware, not crappy plastic sporks that snapped the first time they touched a solid surface.

"So," I began. "Where did Tiara come from? Is it a nickname or your real name?"

Tiara pulled her slit shirt up even further on the left side; a tattoo in the shape of a crown stood out against her creamy skin. "It's actually a birthmark. I thought it was cool, so I had it gone over with ink to make it permanent."

"Very cool," I approved. "Orion has a neat birthmark too."

"Really?" Tiara said, though I was pretty sure she'd already noticed. His birthmark wasn't as easy to hide. I tapped my cheekbone; Orion turned his face toward her, tilting his chin down to give her a better view. She fingered his freckles lightly, tracing the shape of the constellation on his cheekbone. The others leaned forward too.

"Very cool," Tiara repeated. She kept her hand on his cheek for a second too long, not that it mattered to me. Both Orion and Meisha were devastatingly good-looking, but I wasn't interested. No spark. I was pretty sure the universe was laughing at me, because I did have a spark with someone else: Cobalt. Like I didn't have enough problems already.

Scipio served himself gravy from the crock in front of us, and he bumped it a little too hard. Definitely intentional. If it had worked out the way he had intended, the bowl would have fallen over the lip of the table and spilled straight into my lap.

With dragon-enhanced reflexes, my hand shot out to steady the dish and scooted it out of harm's way. "Careful," I said sweetly. "Wouldn't want to spill anything."

Scipio made a face. "Yeah," he said sarcastically.

Cobalt glared. "If you have anything to say, get it out now," he growled. I leaned back and crossed my arms, curious to hear what petty grievances they would use as excuses.

"Nothing to say," Scipio mumbled, echoed by Ice.

"If my brother trusts you, so do I." Micah made his opinion explicitly clear.

"I don't have a problem with any of you," Aimery said, calmer than I'd seen him yet.

"You don't have a problem with anyone," Scipio observed. He sneered down his nose, like we couldn't guess what he thought of Aimery's low standards.

"I don't have a problem with you guys, either," Tiara seconded. She glared a silent warning to Scipio, who shrugged loosely. As she spoke, her eyes shifted to Orion and back.

With our opinions out for all, we settled down to eating.

This is good, Stellar remarked contentedly. Her voice was muffled; it was the mental equivalent of talking with your mouth full. *And you have excellent dinner company.*

You're kidding, right?

She made a sound akin to a dragon snicker. *In manner, not so pleasant. In looks, exceedingly so.*

I choked; Cobalt tapped the small of my back, rubbing in slow circles. "Are you okay?" he asked in concern.

I nodded, gasping; I scrubbed at my watery eyes with the heel of one hand. "Fine," I managed. Stellar must have looked through my eyes, which was something we rarely did. Her curiosity must have been killing her to push her that far.

I was happy, because Stellar was. From the looks on Orion and Meisha's faces, their dragons were as well. A rider is never fully content unless their dragon is, too. I watched them laugh and smile, chatting animatedly with Aimery and Tiara, the two who let us in unreservedly. I smiled too. I had what every leader wanted: a safe, happy, well-fed team. But how long would it last?

Chapter Twenty-Seven

I yawned, popping my jaw painfully. I felt like an anaconda, my jaw stretched so far.

I was tucked between Stellar's forelegs, seated crisscross on the itchy straw of the barn floor. Her heavy wedge-shaped head rested across my knees. I stroked her lightly, from muzzle to crown. Her eyes were closed. She purred in contentment, chest rumbling against my legs. Cool, diamond-hard scales scratched my back as Stellar shifted into a more comfortable position, rustling her wings.

She hadn't said a word in my mind since dinner, when we'd eaten a savory feast of fried chicken, au gratin potatoes, and several slices of pie. Unlike when we had a fight, when the silence in my mind was deafeningly loud, this was a food-induced contentment.

Stellar shifted suddenly, pinning me in place with a wide paw. Her serrated claws were sheathed, which I was glad of. She flopped onto her side with a dull thud, twisting carefully, so that I was barely jostled. I curled up next to her, basking in the warmth of the hidden fire in her belly. Stellar swept her vast black wing over me like a tent, and when I closed my eyes, it wasn't any darker. I sighed deeply in contentment and dropped off to sleep.

Stellar huffed in irritation. I jerked awake abruptly, careful not to allow my breathing pattern to give me away. The last thing I wanted was to alert the intruder to the fact that I was awake.

He's here, Stellar informed me sourly.

He who? I demanded.

Cobalt.

"Damn," I said aloud. I tapped Stellar's wing lightly, asking her to lift it so I could crawl out. She obliged lazily, not bothering to stand. Apparently having decided I could handle him on my own, she huffed and tucked her muzzle back under her wing, her serpentine neck winding in a way that was impossible for anything else.

Cobalt leaned against the wall next to our stall's open door. I clicked my fingers together gently. He whipped his head around, face loosening in relief. I crooked my forefinger at him, sliding to the side so he could enter the stall with me. Steel, who had never accompanied Cobalt before, planted himself in the doorway. His bulk contained what heat there was in the barn, as well as the added bonus of giving us our privacy. He extended his muzzle to Stellar, who peeled her head out from beneath her wing to meet him.

I slid down the wall next to Cobalt. To my surprise, Stellar extended a wing across both of our laps, like a quilt made of thin membranes. We sat so close our shoulders and knees touched. I told myself it was only because it was so cold in here.

Cobalt cleared his throat roughly. I waited patiently for him to speak, knowing, or at least reasonably sure, that he wouldn't have trekked out to the dragon barn from wherever he slept for no reason. "I've been thinking," he began.

"Uh-oh," I cracked, trying to lighten the mood. It worked- somewhat.

He grinned weakly. I shifted closer, surprised at how vulnerable he looked. I was also surprised that my first instinct was to comfort him, not to make a smart-aleck comment, which would be the typical teenage response. "What's on your mind?"

He stroked his fingers through his hair, skimming it back from his high forehead. He sighed shakily. "I was just thinking," he repeated. "About all the stuff each of our projects knows that they haven't shared with the other. How much better off would we and our dragons be if they just forgave whatever enmity that they have and partner up?"

"A lot," I admitted. I would like nothing more than for us to work together, but the first step would have to be letting us go, which I didn't foresee happening anytime soon.

"Come on," Cobalt said suddenly, taking his turn at lightening the mood. He grabbed my hand and towed me up. Stellar grumbled at having to shift her wing. He motioned impatiently for Steel to move, and the dragon did, with a grumble almost exactly like Stellar's.

Cobalt tugged me out of the barn, treading lightly so we didn't wake Orion. We stood on opposite sides of the sliding door and heaved, him pushing and me pulling, waiting with bated breath to see if the rollers would squeal and give us away.

He pulled me along, half-jogging, to what I assumed was the other dragon barn. And right past it, to a squat shed. The outbuilding was low and gray, with a tan sliding door at the front and a side door tucked into the gray paneling.

Cobalt removed his dagger from the sheath, the first time I'd seen it. It was thicker than mine, but no longer. He slipped the point into the lock and wiggled it back and forth, tapping it occasionally with his palm. Taking too long; I'd have liked to get some sleep that night.

"Move over," I whispered. I tugged a bobby pin out of my belt loop, where I always put them if they weren't in my hair. Two of the picks were devoid of the tiny blobs that prevented them from catching on hair. Painful, if I forgot and put them in, but so worth it. Two deft flicks; the lock clicked. "After you," I whispered, bowing sarcastically and stepping out of the way so Cobalt could enter first. This was his idea, after all.

The dragon nearest to the door snuffled and lifted her head. She was curled up like a snake. She uncoiled herself and stood. I sucked in a breath, terrified that she was going to decide to eat us, or possibly worse, get us caught. Instead, she extended her dainty muzzle toward me, and I cupped my palms to meet her. Her warm breath fluttered against my fingers.

The dragon was a mix of violet and lavender, with fox-red freckles from her nostrils to the ridge between her eyes and bright red rings around both of her eyes. Personally, I thought she looked like a paint-splashed raccoon, but her temperament more than made up for it.

"This is Orianth," Cobalt introduced, patting her muzzle. She allowed it, but shuffled a step closer to me and pressed her muzzle into my collarbone.

"Hello, Orianth," I whispered, scratching her on the soft scales under her chin, feeling them scrape against my trimmed nails. She bent her head and closed her teeth around my hand. My heart stuttered, until I realized the only thing tightened around it were her soft lips. She tugged me forward and flopped down onto her side, offering Cobalt and me something to lean against.

We sat down in almost the exact same position as before, except that her wing... I gasped.

"Where are her wings?" I said shakily. Cobalt snuck a quick look up.

"She doesn't have any," he answered, sounding puzzled.

That puzzled me. "Why not? Was there an accident?"

He shook his head and hurried to explain. "No. She's a breeding dragon. She never had any."

"Do any of them?" I asked, glancing around at the nest of dragons around us.

I'd been so preoccupied with Orianth that I hadn't even bothered to take a look around. Dragons of all shapes and sizes curled up on thick cushions like mattresses; all of them were fast asleep. Their chests and sides rose and fell rhythmically, and their tails flicked in dreams. None of them had wings, now that I looked.

There was also a nest of blankets piled in the far corner of the shed. Tiny dragons, which I assumed were quite young, peeped out from the thick pile. Quilts and heated blankets, heaps of stuffing and flat pillows, made up the stack. Snaky heads popped out, surveyed us, decided we weren't worth leaving the warmth, and slid back in.

"No," I answered my own question.

"Do you know why she's colored like this?" Cobalt asked, stroking Orianth's haunch. I wasn't sure if that was a trick question, but it was clear he expected an answer, so I gave him the best one I could think of on short notice.

"She's a twin," I said confidently. Coach had always said be confident, whether it's the right answer or not.

"What does that have to do with anything?" Cobalt asked. I realized suddenly that he didn't know. His pose, leaning forward, elbows on knees, staring intently, wasn't one that suggested he knew the answer.

"Dragons lay a bunch of eggs to fool predators; only a few of them actually hatch. Twins are ones that hatch from the exact same egg." I tilted my head, trying to remember anything else I'd been told on this particular subject. "Something about their genetics changes because they shared an egg. Nutrients, or something like that." I shrugged sheepishly. "I wasn't really paying attention when they explained it to me."

"Surprise, surprise," Cobalt teased.

I punched his arm lightly, surprised at how at ease I felt with him. It was a sudden thing, and not a rational one. When we'd arrived, I'd been so angry; I would have done anything to escape (which I'd proven by punching Cobalt in the face). If I wasn't careful, I might even want to stay.

"Well, can you blame me? I had just found out that dragons existed. Dragons! I was so ridiculously happy," I shot back.

He held up his hands in surrender. "I don't blame you," he defended. "I was the exact same way when I came here."

"I was kind of obsessed with dragons when I was a kid," I admitted, like that explained everything.

He nodded understandingly, his thick black hair flopping on his forehead. "So was I."

I made a face. "My mom cured me of that. Imagine my surprise when I found out she was wrong. Ha!" I barked a laugh. "It was a fairly rare occurrence. Not that I could tell her anyway."

"Do you want to?" he asked, scrunching his dark brows together.

I considered. "No. She'd only turn it against me, like she does with everything else."

He chuckled gently. "A little bitter, aren't we?"

I shrugged. "Maybe."

Orianth rolled her head out of my lap, pulled back, and slurped her long tongue over my face, from chin to forehead. The hair on my forehead stuck straight up; I felt like a unicorn, even as I tried to scrape it back down.

Cobalt leaned even closer. "You've got dragon spit," he said seriously. If it had been anyone but me, I would have been laughing my butt off at whoever was unlucky enough to be slobbered by a dragon. Either he was a better person than I was, or something else was going on here.

The pad of his thumb swiped off my lip; he leaned closer. Before I realized what he was doing, his thumb was replaced by his lips. His mouth was warm and soft. All I could think of were problems: I had dragon spit all over my face, my breath probably smelled like sour cream & onion chips (which I'd eaten for dinner), or that my lips were chapped. I picked my lip when I was nervous, the equivalent to most people chewing their fingernails.

Orianth huffed, something akin to laughter. Cobalt and I pulled away like someone had dumped ice water on us. My face flamed red; Cobalt's was a red that would have made a bull see, well, red.

I stood quickly, eager to get away from him. It hadn't been a bad kiss, from my limited experience, but looking like he did, he probably had far more to compare it to. What if I'd done something wrong? What if he hadn't liked it? Not like I could ask him!

"Night," I mumbled. I kissed Orianth lightly on the crown and fled.

Chapter Twenty-Eight

I refused to look Cobalt in the eye the next morning when he escorted us to breakfast. I spoke in monosyllables and attempted to keep Meisha and Orion at arm's length. I wasn't really all that hungry, which Stellar, and everyone else, noticed; everyone but Ice and Scipio, who apparently didn't care, commented. I ate just to give me an excuse to shrug and wait for them to move onto the next topic.

What's wrong with you? Stellar demanded in irritation, nearly decapitating me with her wing as she wheeled overhead.

Since we still weren't allowed to leave the barn except for meals (something I'd complained about numerous times) we'd taken to doing drills inside. The dragons swooped overhead, giving us ample practice in dodging projectiles. They got a little too into it, if you ask me.

We would run up and down the aisle, throw the bales of straw that served as bedding, and spar. Finished with wheeling overhead, our dragons would lie in the loft, tails flicking, and knock hay bales off onto our heads. Believe me, you look up quick.

Cobalt escorted us back from dinner that night. After three days of trying to figure out why Cobalt had kissed me, I'd given up. I'd convinced myself that it didn't mean anything, otherwise why wouldn't he have repeated it? And so resolved never to mention it again.

The boys had run ahead to the barn, chasing each other and whooping; Cobalt and I walked in companionable silence. Our dragons watched from the mouth of the barn, lying side by side.

Cobalt cleared his throat. "I have good news," he started.

"Oh?" I said warily. One thing that could be said for the kiss, other than that it was completely baffling, was that it had served to reopen my eyes to the fact that we were prisoners. Maybe we were well fed and had a space of our own to defend against the vicious glares; maybe the leaders were starting to warm up to us, except Micah, for some reason. But we were nonetheless prisoners. We needed to start looking for a way out.

"My bosses have agreed to let you three train with us each day," he said. "Your dragons will be allowed to fly, with supervision, for three hours per day."

"Cool," I said sincerely. After all, we'd need to be in shape to pull off an escape from this many dragons. It was a longshot at best, but we had to try.

"Look," Cobalt blurted; he looked like he regretted it almost instantly. "About the other night..."

"What about it?" I said warily.

"I just wanted you to know..." He raked his fingers savagely through his hair; it looked like he ripped out a few strands.

"Wanted me to know what?" I said coolly. On the exterior, I was channeling the ice queen; on the inside I was screaming *Spit it out already!* at the top of my lungs.

"It was great," he blurted. "But I don't want you to think that you have to do anything."

"I don't," I assured him. Yet again, he had managed to turn my world upside down. Again I was confused. Did I really want to leave? Or should I stay?

I stretched up on my toes and planted my lips on his. I admit, and I am not exactly proud of this, but it wasn't exactly purely motivated. For one, if he could spring something like that on me, I could do the same to him. For another, I was pretty sure my dagger was still tucked through the belt loops of his jeans. When I kissed him, tilting my head for a better angle, he didn't even notice my fingers sliding it out and dropping it into my boot. Sheathed, luckily.

He pulled away. "Good night," he managed huskily.

"Good night," I repeated.

Chapter Twenty-Nine

I swallowed a bite of bacon and refilled my glass of orange juice. "Pass the toast, please," I called to Tiara. She was halfway down the table from me, nearest to the toast.

She obliged, arm shaking slightly as she extended the heavy porcelain platter. I plucked a golden brown piece off and thanked her; Aimery passed me the dish of butter before I even opened my mouth to ask. I thanked him too and slathered on a chunk of butter.

The door to the hall slammed against the stone wall. We all glanced up, mouths full. Military man, who Cobalt had later told me was actually named General Mafector, stood stiffly. His arms remained folded behind his olive fatigues as he stalked up the aisle.

The tapping of his army boots ceased as he halted in front of our table. "Cobalt," he rumbled. "You need to come with me."

Like the mostly obedient soldier he was, Cobalt stood immediately.

"Wait," Micah said, holding up his hand. "Why?"

Mafector's eyes glinted maliciously as he stared down his nose at Micah. "You are not in the 'need to know'," he sneered coolly. "I'm not permitted to provide you with that information."

My eyes narrowed as Micah opened his mouth to speak furiously. "Hey." When he turned to look at me, I did what I do best: annoy people.

"Could you possibly be any more pompous? He asked you a simple question, one that we would all like answered," I grinned. My smile was as sharp edged as my dagger.

He sneered, no longer bothering with his thin facade of respect. "You definitely don't need to know, girl," he scoffed.

I bristled, drawing up to my full height, as much as I could without leaving my seat. Cobalt stopped me cold. "Leave it," he ordered. "It'll be fine." I closed my mouth with a mutinous glare at Mafector. I was doing this only because Cobalt had asked me to.

He followed Mafector up the long aisle, accompanied by stares from all sides, and out the double wood doors. For some unfathomable and worrying reason, it looked like a death march to me. I couldn't shake the feeling that everything would be changed by whatever happened next.

Chapter Thirty

I t had been several days since Cobalt had left the hall with Mafector, and I hadn't seen him since. We were escorted to and from meals by a silent mountain of a rider with flaming red hair. He wasn't overly aggressive, but neither was he outwardly friendly. He wasn't anything at all, really. Just a flat face and no inflection in his voice when he spoke to us, which wasn't often.

When I asked the others at the leader's table, they assured me Cobalt was probably perfectly fine. He may have been out on a mission. It could have been a surprise performance assessment, which he would no doubt pass with flying colors. Aimery even gently suggested that he might have taken a vacation. I sincerely doubted that, though it would fit with his continuous pattern of baffling me.

I couldn't shake a bad feeling. No matter how hard people tried to convince me that Cobalt was perfectly okay, I just couldn't believe them. Orion, Meisha, Tiara, and well-meaning Aimery all tried their very best to distract me, to no avail. Scipio and Ice just laughed at me, which did nothing to dispel my worries.

We were finally reduced to training together. To our surprise one morning, Tiara and Aimery showed up and wordlessly joined in our training sessions, which meant that not only were we training with them in their training building, a low-slung gray beast with a massive gym and weight room, they were working out the low-tech way, in our barn.

Like I said before: we're organized. Bored one night after dinner, with the boys scratching a game of tic-tac-toe into the straw, I set about cleaning up the barn.

I climbed into the loft and piled the bales in neat stacks, two to a pile. I polished our saddles with a pilfered cloth and organized the first aid kit. I only systematized my own bag, for the boys wouldn't let me anywhere near theirs. I ordered the dragon's grooming kits and groomed them as well. They shone with their respective colors, which left nothing for me to do.

Digging in Stellar's stall for a pebble, dodging her flicking tail, I discovered something strange: a faded, crumpled photograph. Two boys stood grinning with their arms around each other's hips. They looked like twins, with the same shining eyes and heartbreaker grins. They were both blonde; one had long hair, while the others hair was trimmed short and severe. The one with the short hair had round glasses pushed up onto the top of his head. His clothes were starched and carefully pressed; the other wore a faded leather bomber jacket and equally faded jeans. They looked like the two ends of the spectrum: the wild one, and the quiet one.

The photo breathed happiness; the dog-eared edges spoke of fond memories relived many times. I knew for a fact I wasn't mine; I'd never seen it before in my life. Whose then?

I face-palmed as the answer came to me. It had to be Cobalt's; no one else had been in this stall as far as I knew. Who were the men in it? The photo was old; maybe uncles. Too young to be grandparents.

I added the photo to the long list of questions I had to ask Cobalt when I finally saw him again. First and foremost, *where have you been?*

Chapter Thirty-One

As usual, the leaders were already at the table when we arrived. It was lunchtime; the hall was nearly empty. Most Base riders trained at this time; they would straggle in throughout the day to eat the food that the cooks kept warm all day in long steam tables.

I plopped down and filled my plate slowly. I had no real appetite, so I only picked at my food and listened to the conversations taking place around me, rarely taking part. Micah sat across from me, leaning over to laugh at something Tiara had said. It suddenly hit me: there was no doubt whatsoever that the boys in the photograph were related to Cobalt and Micah.

There were differences. Micah's hair was black, not blonde; his features were duller, like a sharp blade that had fallen into disrepair. And yet, they were so similar. They had the same tilt of the head and facial profile; their long noses all had the same distinct Roman arch. Cobalt had that look about him too, but different, like he was, I don't know, another generation or something. It was definitely a puzzle, and I wanted it solved.

I ambushed Micah as he left. Tiara and Orion had snuck off; Aimery was no doubt curled up in a corner somewhere with a book. Ice was probably stretched it out in a patch of sunlight. She was that catty.

"Hey," I called, jogging a few strides to catch up with him. He turned curiously, arching his eyebrows.

"What's up?" he asked warily. Even after all the time we'd spent during meals, talking and chatting and trying to get the other to spill secrets they hadn't intended to divulge, we didn't like each other. A healthy respect, maybe.

I pulled the picture out of my pocket, smoothing it carefully. "Do you know who these people are?" I asked, gauging his reaction carefully.

He shrugged. I knew right away he was going to lie. Too casual, refusing to look me in the eye and then remembering himself. Stellar flew high overhead. She growled. Even though she was a hundred feet above my head, I felt the snarl in my bones, but also in my throat, as if I'd snarled myself. *Do you need me to come down?*

No.

"Some family relation, probably," he said nonchalantly. I nodded, deciding it would do me no good to call his bluff. I filed away the fact that he had blatantly lied to me for later.

"Okay," I said easily. "Just curious." If it really was a relation, then why would he lie? Yet another secret in this massive web of them.

Chapter Thirty-Two

As the days without Cobalt stretched into weeks, our training sessions grew even more intense. We ran harder, fought longer. Hours in the workout room, a short lunch, and we were back to the barn to train some more.

The boys followed my rigid regimen with less zeal than I did, but still did their best to keep pace. They never complained, although I hadn't intended for them to be the ones pushed so hard. I had intended for it to be me; I needed to keep my mind off of the missing Cobalt. The best thing for that was to work out, to push myself so hard that I didn't have time to think.

After a long day of training, with the boys already fast asleep and the others having left hours ago, I tossed and turned. I made up my mind, once and for all, to either escape or find Cobalt, whichever came first.

Stellar did something she hadn't done in a long time; she alerted me to an intruder in the barn. Before I was even fully awake, I had lunged to my feet and out of the stall, and thrown the prowler against the wooden barn wall with my dagger at his throat. A sliver of moonlight flashed through the cracked sliding door and off the thin blade. The attacker swallowed visibly; I felt the motion as it vibrated the dagger in my grip.

At first, my heart leapt; could it possibly be Cobalt? Then he shifted, and my heart plummeted to my boots. Locks of Aimery's thick brown hair drifted forward.

"What are you doing?" I hissed, pulling my dagger roughly away from his throat.

Sorry, he mouthed. Rubbing his throat, he finally recovered enough to speak.

"I'm worried about Cobalt," he said hoarsely, still rubbing his throat.

"So am I." Then I pointed out, "But you, and everyone else, told me I was being paranoid." I crossed my arms over my chest, careful to keep the edge of my blade away from my arm. Our uniforms had recently been returned to us. Micah had hinted that it might not be a good idea to wear them, since it would make us stand out from the crowd of identical uniforms. I'd told him the truth, although perhaps with more of an edge to my voice than was absolutely necessary: we already stood out, so we might as well be comfortable. I could remember Aimery's hearty compliments on our clothing before Scipio had shut him down.

He shrugged sheepishly, scuffing the straw on the floor with the toe of his boot. "I know," he admitted. His big, pale hand raked through his hair, ruffling it up so that it stood like the hackles of an alarmed cat. "But it's been too long. He's never been gone this long before."

"So what do you want to do?" I said, secretly overjoyed, and smug, that someone had finally taken my concerns to heart. About time.

"You guys prepare. Be ready to escape. If something has happened, and this goes south, we'll need to be ready."

It hit me suddenly, even as my mind whirled off with plans to get food and other necessities. "What about the others?"

"No Micah," he said fervently. "He's shady; I've never trusted him." I nodded ardently.

"Tiara is in; Ice is out. She practically stuck her fingers in her ears and walked away trilling when I approached her, which I took as a definite no."

"What about Scipio?" I asked. He wrinkled his nose. His dragon, a maroon beast that was smaller than all of ours, sneezed ferociously, giving his opinion on the subject. The dragon's size brought to mind the breeding dragons Cobalt had shown me, but he had wings. They were thin and delicate, like large, clawed butterfly wings.

"We'll be ready," I assured him.

He nodded firmly and strode quickly out of the barn. I watched him go, and turned to wake the boys. "Guys."

Chapter Thirty-Three

"Do we have everything?" I asked, rustling through my own bag to ensure I had all the necessities. Affirmatives from the boys. I tossed my bag to Meisha and grabbed Orion's to check.

Meisha held it gingerly. "Is there anything, umm, feminine, in here?" he asked nervously.

I couldn't figure out whether to laugh at him or be offended. "Is this really the time?"

The boys just looked at me. I briefly considered being mean and telling them yes, but I didn't. "No," I sighed, snickering under my breath. "Now hurry up, before our escort comes to take us to breakfast."

We riffled through the bags, checking each item off a mental list. "Got everything," I nodded. I tossed Orion his bag.

"What are you doing?" Scipio growled.

"Just checking that we have all our things," I shrugged nonchalantly. "You never know when one of you Base riders will acquire sticky fingers and decide to take it out on the easy targets."

Scipio looked deeply offended by the mere suggestion, which was an added bonus. "We would never do such a thing," he said stiffly. I arched my eyebrows, like, *Really? You wouldn't?*, but let it slide.

"What did you want, anyway?" I asked, yawning theatrically to show

how thoroughly bored I was with this conversation. It was only partly an act.

"I'm here to escort you to the mess hall."

I stood, motioning for the boys to come. They looked up from where they were braiding thin strands of grass (don't ask me why) and padded over to meet us.

At breakfast, we loaded up with even more than our usual boatload of food; all of it was packed with the protein that we would need to attempt any sort of escapade, be it an escape or a rescue mission. I had a deep bowl of parfait, creamy vanilla yogurt topped with strawberries, bananas, blueberries, and granola, as well as a breakfast burrito with scrambled eggs, sausage, and cheese. A slice of white bread toast with melted butter slathered on top occupied the corner of my colorful plate.

"What are you doing?" someone growled. We froze; Aimery didn't miss a beat.

"Going for a walk," he said easily. The guy was tall and thick, resembling a tree trunk wearing a muscle shirt. He nodded and walked on, obviously accepting Aimery's cool-as-cucumber story as the real deal. Aimery and Tiara walked in front of me. Orion and Meisha were on each side.

One thing I had learned from watching too many action movies, that Aimery had apparently been born with, was this: if you act like what you're doing is perfectly legit and acceptable, people will assume it is. Their brains just can't fathom someone trying to pass off anything else in plain sight. We used that theory to bluff our way past eight people, including a security officer guarding the door to a restricted area that Aimery thought might be holding Cobalt, as it was used to contain prisoners.

Aimery nodded respectfully to the guard. "Thank you."

The guard tried one more time to catch us at something we shouldn't be doing. "Are you sure that the General gave you permission to come in here? Because he told me that I wasn't allowed to let anyone enter."

Aimery sighed gustily. "Yes, I'm sure, but if you want to radio him and interrupt his very important meeting, be my guest. It's your job."

The guard shook his head and grunted in dissatisfaction. "I suppose."

He reached down onto his console and swiped his identification card before punching in a four-digit key code. The doors hissed open; we stepped through without so much as glancing back.

"All right," I said under my breath as soon as the doors whistled closed behind us. "Now what?"

Aimery drew his vined-knife, which surprised me. "Okay," I muttered, stooping to slide my own dagger out of its sheath in my boot. "Straight on to the weapons section of our programs then."

"We need to figure out where Cobalt is. If anyone approaches you, bluff them. If you can't bluff them, take them out of the equation."

"I'll go with Orion," Tiara volunteered. I arched a brow at her as the boys turned aside to discuss strategy; she made a face at me, but grinned good-naturedly.

"That leaves us," I said. As Tiara and Orion started to walk away, I had an epiphany, which let me tell you, is not a common occurrence. "Wait," I hissed. They returned the group, grumbling. "What's the signal if we find him?"

Meisha piped up. "Make as much of a racket as possible?" I tilted my head and look across to Aimery; he nodded.

"Good enough."

"Let's go find him!" Meisha cheered.

"Meisha!" I hissed. "Have you found him yet?"

He frowned in confusion. "No. Why?"

"Then please, for the love of all that is holy and revered in the world, shut up!"

Chapter Thirty-Four

We encountered no one, which worried me. The sterile white hallways were empty; there might as well have been tumble-weeds rolling over the pristine white tiles.

When Aimery had explained the plan to us, I had understood this place to be a few rooms, a few hallways at most. In reality, it was an entire wing of identical doors. Each required a specific pass code and an identification card; some even required fingerprints.

After a several wrong turns and a hurried duck around the corner to avoid a guard, accompanied by a tirade of near-silent epithets, we found the central hub. It was a desk, the abandoned chair spinning slowly, eerily similar to a horror movie scene. The high front of the desk refused entrance, but we vaulted the half-door on the side. We assumed the desk was manned, and that the occupant had only temporarily left, so our riffling through the stack of papers was hurried and messy.

It was ridiculously easy to find the codes to the doors; I I scribbled them onto a Post-it note and hissed at the boys to hurry up as footsteps clicked down the hall.

Boys being boys, they completely ignored me until it was too late. We dove under the desk, breathing shallowly and jostling for space. We were all fairly tall, so the scant space under the desk may as well have been a cage. None of us had enough room, but we didn't dare move because the desk's occupant had returned. The secretary, a woman, plopped down on the desk chair; it gave an alarming whoosh and sank down several inches.

Her chubby ankles shifted forward an inch; the heel of her pointy stiletto sank down onto the top of my foot. The boys only just managed to put their hands over my mouth before she heard my pained yelp; we had to rearrange and cover Meisha's mouth when she rolled the chair over his hand. Couldn't she just sit still?

I guess she must have forgotten something, because she rolled her chair back and stood up. We listened to her footsteps receding for a few seconds. As soon as we were sure she was gone, we peeled out from under the desk and bolted. I don't think any of us really picked a hallway or even a direction to run; we just got as far away from the clumsy secretary as we possibly could.

We ran past the first door we needed to check. I skidded to a halt and ran back.

"What are you doing?" Meisha panted. I tugged the codes out of my pocket and typed one in, and the door hissed open. We all peeked around the corner, probably looking like a stupid cartoon, to find: an empty room. We sighed collectively and pulled back. I thought the file said the rooms whose codes I hacked were occupied? Either they needed to update their files more regularly or something strange was going on here.

It took us a dangerously long time to check all of the rooms. Each was empty; most looked like they hadn't even been used for a long time. Each had a low cot with a thin blanket, a nightstand topped with an empty pitcher and glass, as well as an adjoining room that I assumed was the restroom. The nightstand was dusty, and the pitcher and glass needed to be cleaned before they could be used. There were tiny tumbleweeds of dust bunnies on the drab gray tile.

The last room was halfway across the wing; we walked slowly, already exhausted from stress. Our rapid adrenaline rushes weren't helping. Every time we thought we heard a security guard, we'd dive for the nearest hiding spot, often hitting each other in the process; we waited with bated breath to see if our ears had been correct. Thankfully, most of the time they weren't.

I typed in the code for the last door: four-eight-one-nine-nine-nine. The door hissed open the same as the others, with one major difference: this one was occupied.

"Cobalt!" I hissed. He lay on his side on the cot, back to the door. When I spoke, he twisted around, jaw dropping when he saw us. Once they knew he was okay, the boys ran to find the others; we had revised our early plan of noise-making for fear of it being too risky. I informed Stellar that we'd found him; she sent back a bright blue lightning bolt, which she often used in place of Cobalt's name.

Cobalt unfolded himself from the cot, rushing across the short space and wrapping his arms tightly around me. He pulled back. "What are you doing here?" he whispered fiercely.

I arched an eyebrow at his tone. I hadn't expected him to be so ungrateful. "I was worried. And so were the others," I added hurriedly, not wanting to take all the credit.

"Ice probably wasn't," he snorted. "Who else is here?"

I ticked our number off on my fingers. "Orion, Meisha, Aimery, Tiara and I."

He nodded slowly, eyebrows scrunching as he mulled that over. "No Micah either?"

I shook my head. I wasn't sure of how to tell him that we didn't invite his brother because we didn't trust him, so I stayed silent. "That's not surprising. Although it would have been easy for him to keep up the charade by coming along. Or even leading you guys in the wrong direction and keeping you from finding me." He wasn't talking to me anymore; he raked his fingers through his thick hair, the ink black strands tangling around his fingers. It looked like it hadn't been brushed for a while, which was atypical of him. Then again, he probably wasn't provided with beauty products in solitary confinement.

"What are you talking about?" I asked warily. I had a sneaking suspicion of what his irritated mumblings meant, but there was no way I was going to accuse his brother of anything before he explained the whole situation to me. Or what he knew.

"Micah is the one that's been keeping me here," he admitted, staring off into the air just above my shoulder.

"And why would he do that?" I asked slowly, trying to keep my voice calm. When he wouldn't look at me, I grabbed his chin gently and pulled his face around. "Cobalt, why?"

"It's not your fault," he mumbled, still refusing to make eye contact.

I went cold, like someone had dumped ice down my shirt. "What isn't my fault?"

He sighed and lifted his chin, his blue eyes meeting mine slowly. "He has a secret to keep."

"That's right, I do," a voice agreed. I flinched, shifting to stand in front of Cobalt. He gripped my shoulders gently and pulled me back so that we stood shoulder to shoulder, which I appreciated. Most guys would have put me behind them out of a misplaced sense of chivalry. Cobalt didn't, though I wasn't sure if it was because he genuinely thought I could handle myself or if he didn't care about me. Still.

"And what would that be?" I asked cautiously.

He feigned surprise, putting his hand to his chest as if he was shocked. "It wouldn't exactly be a secret if I went around telling everybody, would it?"

"Then don't expect me to care," I snapped hotly. My hand slid into Cobalt's; I tugged him forward a step before he refused to proceed any further. "We're leaving," I warned. The warning was for both Micah, who was blocking our path, and Cobalt, who still refused to budge.

"Tell her, or I will," Cobalt said coldly. "She deserves to know."

Micah arched an eyebrow. "I wasn't aware you cared about her that much."

"Neither was I," I muttered under my breath.

Cobalt's mouth quirked, but his eyes never left his brother. "Tell her," he repeated.

"That picture you found," Micah sighed. "Do you still have it?"

I glanced at him sidelong. "Of course." I pulled the photo out of the hidden pocket in the wrist of my uniform. We had hidden pockets everywhere in our uniforms. They did occasionally come in handy, like right now.

I smoothed the picture carefully and handed it to Cobalt, intentionally ignoring Micah's reaching hand, as much of a snub as I was willing to risk right now.

"What is this about?" I questioned.

Cobalt pointed to the boy on the left, the troublemaker. "Does anything stand out about him to you?"

I rolled my eyes. "Yes, he looks like you guys. I thought we'd already established that?"

"Humor me," he insisted; Micah tilted his head, a smug grin on his face.

"She's not gonna get it."

I huffed indignantly. "If y'all are done insulting my intelligence, I'm going to leave now." *Where, for the love, were the others?* It kind of defeats the purpose of bringing backup if they're nowhere to be found when you need them!

"Please?" Cobalt pleaded. I sighed inwardly, then snatched the photo from him, careful not to rip it. I ran a cursory glance over it, not expecting to see anything more than I had the first time. Imagine my surprise when I did.

The boy on the left, the one with the leather jacket, had a scar. It wasn't a disfiguring, change-your-face-forever kind of scar; it actually gave his face character. It was faded pale even in the photo; whatever caused it must have happened years and years ago. It was low in his chin; if he'd grown a beard it would have been buried and invisible.

I looked at Micah, not quite daring to believe my memory. After all, you hear all those doctors blab on and on about how the human memory isn't infallible, blah, blah, blah. Mine was no exception to the rule.

Except it was. As I'd known it would be, the tiny scar stood out starkly against Micah's strong jaw. When I'd first come to The Base (read: been kidnapped), Micah had a five-o'clock shadow. I'd just always assumed it was to lord the fact that he had facial hair over Cobalt, who wasn't old enough. Something about dragons changes us, inhibits our ability to grow hair.

Now I realized it was to hide the scar; from whom though? If that scar was as old as it looked, there weren't many people at the Base who were even alive back then. Most of us were teenagers. Our older siblings hadn't even been a glimmer in our parent's eyes back then.

"What happened?" I asked, tapping my chin lightly, in roughly the same place. I struggled to hide it, but I was freaking out. Somebody needed to explain this to me soon, or my logic-puzzle-solving-brain was going to explode.

"My brother hit me in the face with a shovel," he said flatly. I blinked. Now I knew why I hadn't wanted siblings. As I realized what he'd said, I held up my hands in a time-out T. "Cobalt hit you in the face with a shovel?" My stomach rolled. I mean, I'd thought about dating older men before, but I never actually had. Even so, twenty-some years older than me is a little more than I could handle.

Micah smirked. "No. Another brother."

I breathed a deep sigh of relief. "I wasn't aware you had another brother," I said cautiously.

"Because it's not exactly something either of us advocates to the general public," a voice said behind me. I jumped and twisted around to look over my shoulder; Hale patted my shoulder comfortingly. "Not that I would classify you as the general public, of course, Miss Chevalier."

I glanced back and forth between the three of them. Yes, they all had certain physical similarities. Good looks for one; I hadn't noticed with Hale because he was, well, quite a bit older than me. Thick hair with a widow's peak, though Cobalt's and Micah's was black and Hale's was a distinguished silver fox shade. Long, straight noses and strong jaws; bright blue eyes, though Cobalt's were, in my opinion, the prettiest. Hale's were sort of washed out, like a favorite pair of jeans that had been washed too many times. Micah's creeped me out; they sort of glittered, which reminded me of a children's book I'd read about an evil gremlin. Micah was quite a bit taller and better looking than the gremlin was, but it was a dangerous, approach-with-caution kind of beauty, like a king cobra. They're beautiful at a distance, but you wouldn't want to cuddle with one.

I looked down at the photo, clenched tightly in my grip. Their hair color was different, but a cheap hair dye would take care of that in an hour.

"Actually, to be clear," Hale explained, touching Cobalt's shoulder lightly in greeting. "Cobalt is our half-brother. Only Micah and I are full brothers."

"How is that possible?" I asked. I waved my hand back and forth between them, hoping to convey several things. The vast difference in age, for one.

Micah snickered maliciously. "You haven't told her? Haven't explained it to her?"

Hale huffed. "Miss Chevalier's training has been primarily functional," he said stiffly. "We saw no reason to burden her with unnecessary information."

Micah barked a laugh, wagging his finger at Hale chidingly. "'Unnecessary information'?" he snorted. "Like the risks she'd be taking?"

My heart stuttered. "What are you talking about?" I interrupted.

Micah waved his hand lazily at Hale, like he was giving him permission to explain. Hale glared, obviously as offended as I would have been, but gestured toward the cot with that genteel manner of his. "If you would sit down, I will be happy to explain."

I plopped down, letting go of Cobalt's hand so I didn't drag him down with me; he sat down anyway. He didn't touch me, which I had mixed feelings about, but until I figured out what the flying flapjack was going on here, everything was on hold.

"Explain."

"When a rider bonds with a dragon, it changes everything. The makeup of your DNA, your body's systems, your mind. Everything," he repeated. "Not the least of these changes is how long you will live. How old do I look to you?"

I blinked at the sudden change in topic, and scrunched my face up. Even to me, this seemed like a trick question, but I decided to be honest. He'd asked, after all. "Maybe early to mid-sixties," I responded warily.

His mouth twisted wryly. "I suppose I did ask," he said, more to himself than anyone else, though Micah snorted. "I'm actually thirty seven, as is Micah."

My jaw dropped; I hurried to yank it back up. I held up my hand as I flushed. "I'm sorry; that was rude of me."

He waved his hand, eyes twinkling. He'd obviously recovered from his seconds-long bout of melancholy. "It's fine. Micah and I are identical twins, actually."

"I can see the resemblance," I said sheepishly, still feeling awful for my reaction.

Laughter rang out, from the other three in the room. I frowned darkly, punching Cobalt lightly in the arm, whose shoulders shook with silent laughter. "It wasn't a joke," I said indignantly.

"We know," Cobalt gasped, patting my leg. I drew away from him with a thunderous frown.

"I apologize," Hale said, reining in his rare show of exuberance. "I realize how you must feel. This is quite a surprise, I imagine."

I nodded vehemently. "So if you're twins, why do you look…" I hesitated, trying to figure out a way to phrase it without seeming as rude as I did before. "Different?"

Hale sighed. "A dragon has an extended lifespan, so, by extension, so will their rider. But if your dragon dies, your aging will speed up hugely."

"So you had a dragon?" I breathed. "That died?"

He nodded sadly. "Sarja. He was my other half, like Stellar is for you." He nodded to Cobalt. "And Steel is for you."

Cobalt winced; he'd obviously heard this story before. I didn't blame him. Even as I reached back to stroke Stellar's muzzle, I couldn't imagine losing Stellar. It would tear me apart. Even the thought of it brought a lump to my throat and tears to my eyes. I blinked rapidly, forcing them back.

I'd gotten so used to Stellar always being at my side that I jumped when my fingers touched the cool wall rather than her slick scales. I could feel her above me when I reached. A part of me always knew where she was.

She reached out to me like she could sense my distress. *You won't lose me*, she promised. *Not ever. I would die to protect you.*

And I would do the same for you, I thought fondly. *But I hope it never comes to that.*

As do I, she agreed. To my surprise, she did what she typically only does at night, before I fall asleep. It felt like a warm quilt was draped over my mind, enfolding me tightly in warmth and love. It made me feel safe and loved. My parents, friends, they'd never made me feel the way Stellar did all the time, and they never could.

"So what happened?" I asked gently. Even that brief brush with Stellar reaffirmed my sympathy for anyone who had lost their dragon.

"I did," Micah said lazily. I whipped my head toward him, face hardening. I'd never liked him, but if he'd killed a dragon, his own brother's no less, there was a good chance I'd go after him. It would also change how I felt about Cobalt, whatever that was. Could I really trust someone with that kind of lineage?

"What are you talking about?" I growled.

"That story you were told, back at Project Rediscovery. Do you remember it?" Hale asked.

I nodded cautiously. "The adult dragon that attacked- and killed- a scientist was his," Hale said, jutting his chin at Micah, who grinned viciously. His straight white teeth flashed as he bowed from the waist with a flourish.

"Sear was always like me," he said fondly. "Quick to rise in anger. I didn't blame him for attacking that scientist."

"But I did," Hale said grimly. "I went after Micah. The dragons caught on and started to fight as well. In the struggle, Sarja's tail clipped me."

"He was knocked unconscious," Micah inserted gleefully.

Hale sent a glare of such absolute loathing his way I fell back against Cobalt in surprise. He wrapped his arms around me lightly, clearly trying to offer comfort but not quite sure how. I patted his hand, resting on my stomach, to let him know that I appreciated the effort. "And?"

"And Sear killed Sarja. He ripped his throat out."

I grimaced. Your dragon being killed was one massively horrible occurrence; knowing that it happened in such a gruesome way was another, even more horrible one. "Go on," I prodded gently.

"By the time the rest of the group got there, all they saw were two adult dragons, one lying dead on the ground, the other standing over a body and two boys, one of which was unconscious. It's no wonder they jumped to the wrong conclusion."

"Except they didn't," I realized.

Hale frowned. "What are you talking about?"

"Well, if Sear killed the scientist and Sarja, it wasn't the wrong conclusion. He really was a killer dragon." I paused, giving my brain a few seconds to process. "But what I don't get is, why didn't they talk about Sarja? The story only mentions one dragon, the killer."

"Because that's all they knew," Micah snorted. "My brother only knows what people told him, which isn't the whole truth. There was a killer dragon, but it wasn't Sear. It was Sarja."

"What are you talking about?" Hale said angrily. "Like you haven't spread enough lies already?"

Micah clucked, an expression of false sympathy on his face. "You didn't know, but the scientist wasn't dead when Sear attacked him. He was still alive when Sear and Sarja fought. At least until Sarja stepped on him, in his death throes." He clicked his tongue, that same understanding expression pasted onto his face. "From what I can guess, it probably crushed his ribs. No one wanted to tell you; you were dealing with the death of your dragon. I certainly wasn't going to tell my perfect brother that his dragon was a killer."

I stood up. "That is enough," I warned, slowly and clearly. "You've told your side, now get out."

He arched an eyebrow at me, folding his arms, the first crack in his facade I'd seen yet. "Brave little thing, aren't you, ordering me out of my own room?"

I glared, crossing my arms to imitate him. "Since you've held Cobalt captive in this room for weeks, I consider this his room," I shot back.

He huffed and turned around, which I suppose was his concession. I turned back to Hale. "How did you even get here?" I asked. Really I was asking, *what took you so long?* but that sounded ungrateful.

He patted Cobalt's shoulder. "He contacted me, at risk to his own life. I have no doubt that he," a pointed glare toward Micah's back, "would have killed Cobalt, and anyone else, to keep this place a secret from me."

Micah laughed and turned back around, spreading his hands benevolently. "Actually, I wouldn't have."

"Don't even deny you've killed people," I said sharply. "I don't doubt it for a second."

He pointed at me; I stood up even straighter, glaring. "I'm not denying that I've killed people, more than you know. But," he held up the finger he'd been pointing at me, "I am denying that I would kill anyone to keep this place a secret from him," a sharp jerk of his chin toward Hale, who stood tall and proud. "In fact," he continued, "I wanted him to find me."

"That's why you kidnapped us," I realized. "Instead of the others who have passed by here on the exact same trip."

Micah nodded enthusiastically, like he was proud I'd figured it out. Chills ran over my skin. It was creeping me out, discussing kidnapping and murder in the same tone you'd use talking about a new muffin recipe. Cobalt slid closer, trying not to be obvious about it. He needn't have bothered, because both Hale and Micah never took their eyes off each other.

"Indeed," Micah agreed. "I heard from a mutual friend that you, picky old man you are, had finally found a candidate to be your spokesperson. That same friend passed on names, descriptions, and when you would be passing by in our neck of the woods."

"I wasn't aware that we had any mutual friends," Hale said haughtily, having finally regained his composure. "Or that you had any friends at all."

Micah shrugged, wagging his finger lightly in his direction. "We have more in common than you know," he chided. Hale's face tightened.

I snorted sarcastically. Micah swiveled his head slowly to look at me; it reminded me of a scene from a horror movie, when the villain turns to look at a victim and then attacks. No matter how ready you think you are for something like that, you never are, but I tensed regardless. "I really doubt that."

Micah opened his mouth to speak, but Cobalt cut him off. "Whatever you want to do, do it," he said coldly. "Don't talk them to death."

I froze at the word, even as his hand tightened on my arm.

Micah pouted, his full lower lip jutting. "You're no fun." *There's that at least*, I thought. *We got to spite a psycho before he killed us.* "But, you're also wrong."

"How so?" Hale asked, having come over to stand by me. I shifted closer to him, my arm just barely in Cobalt's grip, which was loosening slowly.

Micah tapped his chin in thought, even as I shifted closer to Hale, forcing Cobalt to sidle along or risk losing his grip. "Well, maybe you're not," he decided. "I was going to let you," a pointed finger toward me, "live, but you've annoyed me, so I think I might just kill you anyway. And you," this time he pointed at Hale, who glared defiantly, his bushy eyebrows high as he stared down his nose, "were always going to die."

Cobalt shook his head slowly, releasing my arm and rubbing it gently, probably to ease the rapidly bruising skin. "I should have known you wouldn't keep your word," he said slowly. "But I guess I just assumed, because I'm your brother, that it would be different if you made a promise to me."

"Why would it be different?" Micah sneered. "You're not my brother; you're some upstart from our mother's mid-life crisis. The last in a long line of mistakes."

I went white. I know I did; I could feel the color fading out of my face like water draining out of a bathtub. Hale patted Cobalt's shoulder comfortingly, even as he pulled me toward him. I guess he knew I was perilously close to attacking his brother, for no other reason than that last insult to Cobalt. "Don't feel bad," he said. "I am undeniably his brother, and look where that has gotten me."

I winced. *Ouch. Need some aloe vera for that burn?*

Stellar spoke suddenly in my mind and I nearly jumped out of my boots. Judging from Cobalt's nearly imperceptible flinch, Steel was speaking to him as well. *We're on our way. Just stay there.*

We who? I demanded; my temple throbbed with the effort of keeping two conversations straight at once, since Hale and Micah were speaking again. They were using those cold, nearly silent voices that were almost worse than shouting.

We, she responded evasively.

That is not helpful!

Cobalt leaned forward to rest his chin on my shoulder; his breath was warm against my ear. He smelled better than I'd expected. Like, I was stress-sweating and probably smelled nasty, but he smelled like mint and some sort of flowery shampoo. It's always weird when a guy smells girlier than you, but I digress.

"Get ready," he murmured. I dipped my chin imperceptibly, turning my face toward him like I was going to kiss him. Just for appearances, you know.

"Is this the time?!" Aimery yelped. I jumped so hard I heard Cobalt's teeth come together with an audible click. Aimery stood in the doorway, a crossbow bolt aimed at Micah's chest, along with Orion, Meisha, Tiara, and Ice, who had apparently deigned to join us after all. Each carried at least one weapon, if not more, leveled at Micah.

"Don't be such a buzz-kill," Tiara chided. She carried a turquoise recurve bow, a periwinkle arrow nocked and ready to fly. Ice held a dagger, similar to mine, which I'd passed to Tiara when we'd started, because she didn't have a weapon. Actually... it was my dagger, which I would be getting back.

We, Stellar announced proudly. Her muzzle peeked over Orion's shoulder, just barely in view, along with several other dragons. Tyne, Steel, Maath, and several others I didn't know.

"What are you going to do?" Micah snorted. "You're not going to shoot me. I could go through that window this second if I wanted to, and none of you would be able to stop me."

Cobalt tapped the crook of my elbow as he slunk by, and I shifted to block the way. "I would," Cobalt growled, pressing his dagger into his half-brother's back. Micah stiffened, arching his back.

Aimery voiced what we were all thinking: "Now what?"

Chapter Thirty-Five

The door slid closed with a relieved sigh. Or maybe the sigh was me, echoed by the rest of us. From the other side, Micah shouted, pounding on the door. Even though I knew he couldn't get out, I still lunged for the big red button at the bottom of the keyboard. Cobalt's hand slapped on top of mine; the rest piled on within seconds, the top Hale's wizened hand. Cobalt had told us, as we wrestled Micah inside, carefully avoiding his flailing hands and feet but unable to avoid his insults, that the red button was a time lock. Once it was pressed, this door wouldn't open for thirty-six hours unless a fire alarm was pulled. It would stay closed until someone let him out, Cobalt had promised, with a wry and self-deprecating grin. He of all people would know, considering that a cell just like this one had successfully held him for weeks.

Micah's muffled insults were still audible as we walked away. I imagine that was what action heroes felt like, walking stoically away from a fiery explosion. Problem solved.

But I doubted they felt what I did: that there was unfinished business. I just couldn't shake the feeling that I'd missed something, like that answer you remember after you've already turned the test in. You know something is wrong; you just don't know what until it's too late.

We teens celebrated while Hale made some calls, trying to figure out what to do with Micah. We probably couldn't get any charges against him to stick in a real court, but all of us wholeheartedly agreed that something had to be done about him. He needed to be locked up, but we couldn't keep him here forever.

Another thing Hale was working on: what would happen to the Base. As it turned out, Cobalt and I would be getting our wish. Hale was attempting to integrate the two programs; he foresaw a little resistance, but not from the vast majority. It could take weeks, months, or even years, but it would go through.

Parties are too rich for my blood. I've never been a party girl. I don't like people enough to put up with large groups for long periods of time, as illustrated by the bar fight example. I left the party, which was being held in the dining hall, where Hale had explained the situation to the others. They'd sat in silence, which had upgraded to mumbling and whispers, but eventually they'd somewhat wrapped their heads around the idea. As for me, I bailed: headed straight for the place I'd felt happiest here: the shed.

I picked the lock again and snuck in the side door, fumbling around until I managed to find the light switch. Orianth lifted her head, as did the others. I sank down in the cushions next to her; Stellar settled gracefully on my other side, sandwiching me between the warm bulk of two dragons. And then I did what I always do when faced with great stress: I napped.

One thing you discover sleeping in a shed with lots of dragons, most the size of small animals like raccoons or small dogs: in their former life, dragons were housecats. Or, at least, they'd inherited that irritating habit of planting themselves on whatever surface was available to sleep on (say, my head, for example). When I woke up, I expected to breathe clean air, if somewhat tangy because of the dragons' scales. Instead, I nearly sucked a wing up my nose.

I'll admit it: I panicked. I flailed my arms, jerking upright and reaching for Stellar. The smaller dragons, which had been fast asleep on various parts of my anatomy, screeched in protest and leapt away. They flew back to their mound, staring balefully at me with their many sets of indignant eyes. I gasped and rubbed my chest, sucking air frantically. Orianth licked my ankle comfortingly, but ceded the floor to Stellar when she approached. She wove around me, wrapping her tail around my ankles and licking my skin gently.

Dragons have this strange obsession with cleanliness, which extends to their riders as well. Unlike their riders, a dragon's tongue is rough as sandpaper and flexible as a gymnast, to clean dirt out of every nook and cranny. When Stellar had first started to lick my skin, I hadn't been used to it. My skin turned pink and irritated, sometimes even bleeding if she was too rough. Once I'd gotten used to it, her spit had sunk into my skin, making my already pale skin shine like a lantern. I'd noticed the same thing in other riders, though not as pronounced, probably since they were more tanned than I was. I had a ridiculous amount of trouble getting a tan, so I'd given up. I was perfectly fine with my skin tone, so why worry about anyone else? For a fleeting moment, I wondered what Cobalt thought of my skin color, before I shoved it roughly away.

"I should have known you would come here," Cobalt said, his voice laughing, and I looked up to find him smiling at me. "And you've even managed to anger the little demon bats."

"I did indeed." I agreed. I shifted to give him room. Stellar didn't, forcing him to squeeze in between her and me. His shoulder tapped mine as he sat, crossing his legs and accepting Orianth's big head onto his lap. She sighed contentedly when he rubbed the arch above her eyes. I knew the feeling.

"So," I said slowly. "Did you think anyone was going to come after you?"

He tilted his face toward me. "I wasn't actually sure anyone missed me," he admitted shyly.

I gulped hard, trying to swallow the lump of clay that had risen in my throat. "I missed you," I confessed. "After only a couple of days. But the others kept telling me you were fine, and I tried to believe them."

He lifted his head, black hair falling away in a sweep. "But you didn't."

I shook my head gently. "No. I didn't."

He reached out to touch my throat; I flinched. When we'd shoved Micah into the cell, he'd gotten in a few lucky swipes. One on me, three jagged slices on the side of my neck where he'd raked his fingernails down it. Stellar had already cleaned it. I wasn't worried, but it did hurt, especially when someone touched it. "I'm sorry," he said quietly. "I didn't mean for my brother to hurt you."

I shrugged, trying to make light of the situation. "Compared to what he was going to do, it's not that bad." I flinched, clamping my hand over my mouth. Apparently stress also temporarily took my filters out of commission, because that was rude. "I'm sorry," I said, blushing.

He smiled wanly, holding up his hand. "It's fine," he soothed. "I completely agree."

Given that small bit of permission, I was going to take advantage and find out as much as I could. "So you're only half-brothers?" I checked.

He nodded, sliding his hand through his thick black hair, something I did as well. "On our mom's side."

My skin flushed again, but this time from anger. "So that's what that crack was about."

He grimaced and nodded. "You looked like you were going to jump him when he said that."

I smiled viciously. "I was."

"Why?" he asked, tilting his head like a puzzled dog. I felt a little bit bad for him, since he seemed like he genuinely didn't understand why someone would defend him.

I punched his arm lightly; Orianth lifted her head and hissed, but at him, not me, which I thought was hilarious. "Because I'm your friend," I said, like it should be obvious.

A wide grin spread across his face. "You don't have many friends, do you?" I asked, feeling both pity that he didn't and amusement that he reacted that way to something I took for granted. He gave a silent shake of the head, and Orianth licked his hand comfortingly.

I scooted closer, making no attempt to disguise it or be subtle. Our thighs touched; his skin was warmer than mine, even through the material of our uniforms. I'd fallen asleep with my riding jacket on, but I was getting hot, so I peeled it off and tossed it back toward Stellar without looking. It flopped onto her nose; I heard her ominous rumble as she stood. Cobalt looked fascinated as she stood, trudged over to me, tilted her nose, and dumped my riding jacket on my head. I pulled it off, laughing. Stellar laughed as well, her deep rumble vibrating through both mind and body.

Cobalt still looked strangely fascinated, so both Stellar and I turned to look at him. "What?" I asked; the corners of my mouth turned up in an unplanned grin.

He stroked Orianth's head, and she sighed in contentment and licked my knee, which she could only do because I'd scooted closer. "I've just never heard a dragon laugh before," he said wonderingly.

My heart pinched. Stellar shifted, dropping her head between our shoulders, and pressed her broad chest forward so that it touched both of our backs. Very deliberately, she hummed, not quite a laugh, and purred. Orianth caught on, vibrating against our knees.

Cobalt's eyes shone. I couldn't tell if it was tears, or happiness. The latter, I hoped.

I leaned forward slowly, my shoulder scraping Stellar's scaly chest, and pressed my lips to his. His lips were warm and smooth, very different from my chapped, peeling ones.

My mind was pleasantly blank. I was almost buzzing, which I dismissed as happiness until I realized I was buzzing, the dragons' combined happiness rolling over me. Cobalt grinned against my lips; I grinned too, but not enough to pull away.

Suddenly, I jerked away. Cobalt frowned. "What?" he asked breathlessly.

I face-palmed. "I just realized!" I panted.

His frown deepened. "Realized what?"

I hurried to explain. "Earlier, I just couldn't shake this feeling that we were missing something. I just realized what it was!"

His face eased; he'd probably thought my abrupt, skidding halt had something to do with our kiss, which couldn't be further from the truth. "What?"

I held up my fingers, counting off the things I'd thought of so far.

"One, where was Micah's dragon in all this? Better yet, where is he now? Second, who was the traitor?"

"Someone on your side," he mused, clearly choosing to answer the second question first. "Who knew when you were leaving?"

I dismissed that with an offhanded wave. "Everyone. They announced it."

He grimaced. "And the same goes for descriptions, I imagine," he mused. I nodded, flicking my lip with a finger like I always did when I was deep in thought.

"Yeah, but..." I trailed off, pursuing the train of thought, but grimaced. "Nope, no go. I got nothing," I admitted.

He sighed. "Me too."

I sat up straight, and then stood, offering my hand to Cobalt. He took it with a puzzled expression. "Where are we going?"

Stellar peeled herself through the door after us, squeezing her bulk through a doorway meant for something much smaller. "I can't think of anything to eliminate anyone yet, so I figure the easiest way to do that is to see them," I explained.

Cobalt balked, pulling on my hand to stop me; I halted with an irritated sigh. "You mean go back to your side?"

"Technically, I'm the only one going back, because you've never been there." Noticing his crossed arms, I held up my hands in surrender, reluctant to let go of his and so just pulling it along. "Besides, Hale's trying to put them together anyway. I doubt he'll have a problem with us going."

He ran his free hand through his lush black hair. I was strangely happy that he seemed as reluctant to let go as I was. "Don't you mind?" he asked shyly. "Me going with you?"

I shook my head. "I think I had always planned to, ever since we talked about combining the two programs," I said slowly. I hadn't realized, or maybe just hadn't acknowledged that, but as soon as I said it the rightness vibrated through my core. Or maybe that was Stellar's landing; she tucked her wings to her sides and prowled toward the hall with us. "So no, I don't mind," I simplified.

He sighed shakily. "Then I'd be honored to go back with you."

I'm not sure how long it took for me to convince the others that they needed to come back with us. We decided that bringing too many riders at once would overwhelm everyone involved, so a small party of us would go. Cobalt and I would go ahead together, and the others would come the next day. When everyone else would come was up in the air, but it was only a matter of time.

Chapter Thirty-Six

My lungs squeezed like an empty shampoo bottle.

"Air is necessary," I choked out. David squeezed once more before he let go.

"I can't believe you're back!" Cobalt's hand touched the small of my back questioningly. He was too shy to ask about David the bear man. I grabbed his hand and tugged him forward so that he was even with me.

"David, this is Cobalt," I introduced, stepping lightly on Cobalt's toe to encourage him. He jumped and offered his hand to shake. I choked on laughter at how white his face became when David shook. I'd shaken David's hand before; I totally understood.

"Pleased to meet you," David rumbled. "Wait... never mind."

I arched my brows at him, but he waved me away. *Later*, he mouthed.

Cop-out, Stellar complained. Chase approached, and I frowned. Cobalt stiffened, catching my expression out of the corner of his eye. I squeezed his hand gently, but he only relaxed infinitesimally.

"Chase," I greeted pleasantly. He completely ignored me and walked right past.

"Rude," Cobalt hooted under his breath, glaring at Chase's retreating back. Chase's boots crunched green grass as he walked back. "Who are you?" he demanded.

I glared. "A little aggressive, aren't we?" I shot back coldly.

He glared back for a minute, but smoothed his features suddenly. "I'm sorry." Normally I would have accepted that and let it go, but I hadn't trusted him to begin with. Something smelled fishy to me.

"This is Cobalt," I said slowly. Cobalt didn't even try to shake hands; he made no sign to acknowledge Chase's existence, which elicited another glare. "A little hot-cold today, aren't we?" I grinned, intentionally pushing Chase's buttons. I needed to see something, and getting to antagonize him was just an added bonus.

He huffed. "Excuse me," he said rudely, brushing past me.

"Rude," Cobalt repeated. "Who is he?"

I considered naming the things I thought he was, which was a long list of words I would have been expelled for saying. "Some guy," I dismissed. "He's the one they sent to convince my parents to send me here."

"So you must be grateful to him," Cobalt said slowly, his expression unreadable.

I snorted. "Heck no. He's rude, bossy, and arrogant."

He smiled slowly. I thought it was a little too much happiness for something as small as saying that I didn't like another guy, but I'd take what I could get.

"Okay."

Mia approached, her black bob flicking in the breeze. She'd changed all of the pairs of earrings in her ears; more tiny diamonds glittered up and down, which made me wonder if she'd come into recent wealth. If not, where had the money for all these diamonds come from?

"Hey, Mia!" I called. She turned as we jogged toward her; I dragged Cobalt with me for the first few steps before he realized what was going on. He kept up with me easily.

"What?" she asked. Apparently another thing had changed while we were gone: her attitude. She no longer acted like I'd kicked her dragon, which was an even bigger no-no than going after someone's pet; now she acted like I assumed she normally would, to the people she didn't hate, polite and inquiring.

"Could you show Cobalt around?" I asked, putting my hands

together. "I have a few other things to take care of." I saw a flash of that old attitude when she opened her mouth to snap at me; it was quashed when she saw what Cobalt looked like. His black hair was carefully brushed; it hadn't helped much. The thick locks still had waves, like an ocean. His azure blue eyes had dark shadows from lack of sleep. We'd slept in the shed with the breeding dragons last night, curled up with our dragons. Steel had even crept into the tiny building, just as we were about to fall asleep. Like I'd thought, he would let Cobalt sleep under his wing, but he hadn't even thought about it. So that's how we slept: under our dragons' wings, surrounded by the smaller dragons on all sides. For most people, the dark shadows would have made them seem unhealthy and sallow, but for him, it was the equivalent to eye shadow; it highlighted his beautiful eyes, forcing you to look at them and note the unusual color.

"Sure," she said agreeably. Her smile was beatific. I patted his arm lightly and leaned toward him.

"I'll be right back," I promised. He nodded nervously, but padded quietly after Mia.

I ambushed David coming out of the gym. He dropped the staffs he was holding with an unwieldy clatter and put his hand to his heart.

"You nearly gave me a heart attack," he gasped, bending over to catch his breath.

"You're a workout instructor," I snorted. "You'll get no pity from me."

He made a face. "You wanted something," he said, regaining his unruffled exterior.

I nodded. "What did you mean earlier, when you started to say something to Cobalt but stopped yourself?"

He twisted his fingers; I could see him searching for a vague way to answer me. "A real answer," I warned; he grimaced.

"There's a picture of him on Hale's desk," he admitted. "But I wasn't sure what he is to Hale, so I didn't want to embarrass anybody."

I frowned, eyebrows drawing together, until I realized what he meant by that. I opened my mouth to explain and then shut it with an audible click. I couldn't explain, because it wasn't my secret to tell. It would probably come out eventually, but that didn't mean it had to be me who shared. "Yeah," I said vaguely; I waved as I walked away.

"Make sure you start your training again now that you're back!" he called after me; I gave him an overhead thumbs-up without turning around.

Mia and Cobalt sat on the couch in the house, chatting over the loud TV. She was turned toward him, gesturing animatedly, but he was having no part of it. From what I could tell, leaning against the wall and peeking around, trying to seem inconspicuous, he was polite, but not overly interested. He was facing the TV, not turned toward her.

I plopped down on the couch, between the two of them. Mia scooted over to make room. If she had laser eyes, Madame LaVarne would be repairing my uniform, right where my heart is. Since she didn't, all she got was a smug smile.

"You're back," she observed listlessly.

I leaned back against the soft cushions of the old couch, trying to ignore the spring jabbing into my rump. "Indeed I am," I agreed.

Just out of curiosity, I reached for Stellar, pulling the part of my mind that's always aware of her to the fore. It took me a second to realize where she was. I had to reach and see through her eyes to figure it out. She was curled up with Steel on our platform in the Loft, a mix of bright green and ebony black, like a hard-won bruise. They were wrapped up in a tangle of thin wings and long legs; his long pink tongue swiped over a certain place on the dusky gray of her stomach.

I jumped. When we shared like that, which wasn't often (we enjoyed what little privacy we have left), we were basically one. I could feel what she felt, both physical and mental. That brief glimpse made me envious of Stellar, even more than I normally was. Dragons are lucky, in that they don't read too much into every motion and exchange. If they liked each other, they liked each other; end of story. Not like us people.

Cobalt put his hand on my knee lightly; the warmth of his palm leaked through the thin material. "Are you okay?" he asked tenderly. I shifted, closer to him. Not close enough to be uncomfortable, but enough for it to be clear what I was doing.

"I'm just cold," I lied. Following that train of thought, I said,

"Speaking of cold, I think I left my riding jacket in the Loft. I wanted to show it to you anyway; would you like to come with?"

He nodded enthusiastically. "I'd love to," he agreed.

I stepped out the door first, loping easily off the porch and waving to the riders standing there. Cobalt followed smoothly, lengthening his strides to pull even. I wondered what Madame LaVarne would think of their uniforms, nearly all the same. Have a fit, probably.

"So what was that about?" Cobalt asked conversationally. I glanced at him askance. We'd slowed down, enjoying the lush green grass and waving to the passing riders. I'd pointed out the buildings to him, like they'd been pointed out to me when I first came here.

"What was what about?" I asked innocently. He gave me a dry look and waited patiently for me to answer. Stellar wanted to know the answer too, I could tell. I sighed. "I hadn't realized just how closely riders and dragons are bonded." He looked puzzled, so I hurried to explain. "When Steel was licking Stellar earlier, do you know where it was?" He nodded, looking like he still didn't get it. I touched my abs, feeling the ropy scar.

Making a sudden decision, I peeled the bottom of my shirt up, just enough to bare my abs, but no further.

Cobalt sucked air between his teeth. He stared at the scar; even I admit it's pretty BA.

"Where he was licking on her is almost exactly right here," I explained. The ropy scar was pale white, raised at least a centimeter. It stretched from my just under my left rib cage all the way down to my right hip bone. It looked strange where it crossed my abs; I hadn't had abs like that when I'd gotten the scar, so it was quite uncomfortable when I was forming them, skin twisting and warping. And by uncomfortable, I mean really flipping painful.

"What happened?" Cobalt questioned quietly. His fingers touched the ropy scar; I twitched. He froze, even though he must have known it didn't still hurt after all this time.

"Did you know I was a hockey player?" I began. He shook his head, so I continued. I dropped my shirt and spoke as we walked, forcing him to keep up. "Where I trained, the rink... well, it wasn't exactly up to safety standards, but it was an old building, so it didn't have to be."

We'd arrived at the Loft; our dragons swooped down, raining irritated thoughts, to take us to the platform. Finished, Stellar wiped her tongue roughly over my arm and went to join Steel; he waited patiently at the edge of the platform. They winged away; I scooted to the edge of the platform with Cobalt to watch them swoop low and shoot through the partially open sliding doors.

"Where was I?" I mused, much more comfortable telling the story here than anywhere else. It wasn't something I shared very often, after all.

"Something about safety standards," Cobalt provided.

I nodded, twisting a lock of long brown hair around my finger while I thought. "One day, I made a huge mistake. I'd just gotten new skates, so I wasn't used to them. I'd also forgotten my old skates at home. I saw no reason why I couldn't wear the new ones." I snorted. "Big mistake. When I was skating, the toe of my blade stuck in the ice. Nobody realized anything was wrong, so when someone checked me into the wall, no one thought anything of it. Until the glass shattered."

Cobalt flinched, which was pretty much my reaction as well. "I was half over the wall; I think everyone must have assumed I was faking it. When I didn't respond, they all came to look."

"How bad?" Cobalt asked.

"A foot-long shard of glass had impaled me. They called medical transport and took me to the hospital. All in all, a broken wrist, two busted ribs, a dislocated shoulder, a broken collarbone, and internal bleeding. It took eighty stitches and four hours to close the wound; it was another eight weeks before I was allowed on the ice again."

"Any lasting effects?"

"Besides the enormous scar?" I sniped. He grinned and nodded. "My shoulder will never be right again; the pins in it see to that. Sometimes I have trouble breathing because of my ribs, I'm missing my appendix and a few other organs, and my collarbones are uneven. That's pretty much it," I finished. "It could have been a lot worse."

"I'm sorry," he said sincerely, resting his hand on my knee for a second.

"I'm not," I said easily. "So, what do you think about," I made a wide, all-encompassing wave of my arms, "this?"

"I love it," he said after a second. "But I have a few questions to ask."

"Shoot," I said immediately. My bullet wounds twanged at the very mention; I bent over with a breathless half-laugh. Cobalt must have figured out what the problem was, and he grinned.

"Who made your saddles?"

It took me a second to remember their names; I'd heard it only in passing. "Tanya and Andrea," I answered. "Why?"

"Your saddles are better than ours," he explained. I nodded understandingly and made a mental note.

"We'll have to talk to them, see if they can do anything. Next question."

"What happened to your hip?'

I blinked, frowning in confusion. "What are you talking about?"

He reached across and touched my left hip; I peeled my shirt up. "It's just my birthmark," I explained. "I've had it forever."

The birthmark wasn't nearly as cool as Orion's or Tiara's; I would never have it tattooed. A russet sunburst, swirling eternally just above my left hip bone, like an optical illusion.

"It's cool," he said shyly.

I flushed. "Next."

He dropped the subject, to my relief, though his eyes lingered on my hip for a second longer. "Who made your uniforms? Are they all different?"

"Madame LaVarne and yes," I listed. Another entry on the mental list. "We'll talk to her."

"Why don't we do that now? My other questions can wait."

I burst out laughing. "You see, that could be a slight problem," I gasped.

He frowned; the side quirked up while he waited for me to compose myself enough to answer. "The only way to get up to, and down from, the highest platforms is on dragon back," I grinned. He leaned forward, staring at the drop to the floor, looking a little green. Afraid of heights, maybe? Not exactly a great trait for someone who rode dragons, who flew easily as high as a plane, if not higher.

I shivered. The air in the barn was cool, for the same reason the one at the Base was. It wasn't a problem when I was curled up next to Stellar, who was a furnace compared to the cold air. The freezing metal of the platform seeped through my riding pants; I shifted uncomfortably.

I stood and went over to my cot, which I had never used. Why would I, if I could lie next to Stellar? Two thin, navy blue blankets were folded neatly on top. I grabbed them and hugged them to my chest. I also grabbed my riding jacket. I slid my arms through the sleeves of my jacket and gestured for Cobalt to stand. He did, stepping back with a puzzled frown that shifted to understanding when I spread the blanket out where we'd been sitting. We plopped back down side by side. I spread the other blanket around our shoulders and scooted closer to stay as warm as possible.

"I guess we're just going to have to wait for the dragons to come back and get us down."

Cobalt shrugged easily; his shoulder scraped mine. "I'm cool with that."

Chapter Thirty-Seven

I t took the dragons two hours to come back from their flight and help us down from the platform. We spent the entire time talking, answering questions for each other. The blanket stayed wrapped around our shoulders, but we still had to scoot closer for warmth. I'd never noticed how cold the barn was before, and I'd also never realized how spoiled I was because of Stellar. The dragons had a good laugh at us, huddled together for warmth and unable to get down. Whatever; I'd been dealing with that sense of humor for a while now. I could handle the occasional moments of snarkiness, and I couldn't imagine what it was like to deal with me every day.

I tapped the door to Madame LaVarne's workshop. She pulled the door open; her face lit up when she saw me.

"Alex, mon Cherie!" she warbled. "How are you?"

"I'm great," I said sincerely. And why wouldn't I be? Only the fact that there was a traitor in our midst, which I was attempting not to think about until we could figure out something that would help.

She gripped my arm and pulled me in; Cobalt tagged along behind my right shoulder. "And who is he?" she purred. "Someone special?" She winked. I choked; my response ended up being half-shrug and half-shaking my head no, which she thought was hilarious. "Nothing to be ashamed of," she whispered. Then, switching to normal volume, she asked, "What can I do for you?"

"You've heard that the other dragon project is being combined with us?" I asked. She nodded, fiddling with the measuring tape wrapped around her waist like a belt; another was flipped around her neck and over one shoulder like a scarf. "Well, those guys... almost all of them have the same uniform. I was wondering if you'd make new ones for them."

She put her hand over her mouth; she was appalled, like I'd expected. "How many of you are there?"

I looked to Cobalt, whose lips moved; I assumed he was going through the ones he knew in his head. "Probably at least fifty," he guessed. "If not more."

Madame LaVarne still had her hand over her mouth; her eyes shone. "It would be my pleasure," she said, her voice thick with emotion. I hadn't realized it would make her this happy; all the better if it did. I hadn't spent a lot of time with her, but I wanted to change that. What little time I had spent with her was enough for me to decide I liked her.

"I'll leave you to it," I said, backing toward the door. "But before I go, do you know where I can find the women who make the saddles?"

She pointed down the hallway and to the right, already unwrapping her measuring tape. For the first time since we'd arrived, Cobalt actually seemed comfortable. He waved as I slipped out the door and closed it behind me.

The women were hard at work, as I'd expected. Their workshop was as unorganized as Madame LaVarne's was ordered. Leather of various shapes and sizes was stretched over the long trestle tables and flopped on every surface. Sharp tools were laid out on a cushion. Saddles hung on the walls; others sat on racks. Two rolling desk chairs were discarded in the corner, as the women themselves were standing.

They bent over tables, scraping away at leather strips to carve symbols into them. Their faces were scrunched up in concentration. Clear goggles protected their eyes from flying chips of leather. Other strips waited their turn in piles next to them.

Apparently they hadn't heard me open the door, so I knocked force-fully, even though it was a little late for that. They jumped. The blonde, furthest from the door, went back to work, while the brunette approached me.

"What can I do for you?" she asked gruffly. As I'd remembered from the only other time I had heard her speak, her voice was deeper than I'd expected, a gravelly contralto.

"You've heard that the other project is joining us?" She nodded impa-tiently, and I felt a twinge of annoyance that everyone already knew. "I was wondering if you'd make saddles for them. Theirs aren't nearly the quality of you guys'."

I figured a little flattery wouldn't hurt; I was right. She drew up, puffing her chest out for a second before she crashed back down to Earth for business. "How many are there?"

I made a so-so gesture to show that I wasn't sure. "We think about thirty, but only one is here right now. The others will be coming eventu-ally," I responded.

She nodded and walked over to the other woman; they spoke in undertones for a minute before she returned. 'We can do it. Send them in."

"He's being measured for his uniform right now, but I'll send him later."

She nodded and turned toward her work before she remembered her manners. "Is that all?"

I nodded, deciding not to push her any further. One of the women, I wasn't sure which, was famous for her temper. I wasn't particularly anxious to find out if it was her or not. "Thanks."

I sat on the stool outside Madame LaVarne's workshop before I decided to go outside and see Stellar, who lay on the ground just outside the door. I stretched out between her forelegs, deciding Cobalt could probably find his way out by himself. It wasn't that big, right?

Wrong. Stellar poked me with her muzzle, nudging me awake. *What?*

Steel says Cobalt is lost.

I sighed. *'K. I'll find him.*

I went back to the last place I saw him and basically just wandered around.

I ended up in a small hallway, with lots of doors that I assumed were storage or supply closets. "Cobalt!" I called. "Where are you?"

His response was muffled. "In here!" I followed the sound of his voice to the far end of the hall, and jiggled the knob. It didn't budge; I pulled a bobby pin out of my hair and picked the lock. The door swung open and brought me face to face with him.

"What happened to you?" I asked, raising my brows.

"Someone shoved me in here and locked the door!" he said indignantly.

I frowned doubtfully. "Are you sure it didn't just swing shut behind you and lock?"

"I'm sure," he said firmly. He frowned at me, clearly upset that I didn't believe him.

"Okay," I surrendered, holding my hands up. "Let's go."

I showed him to the door and led him and Steel back to the women who made the saddles, explaining that Steel needed to be measured. I waited on a stool in the corner, fingering a piece of silver that was in the process of being affixed to the chest piece of another saddle, just to keep my restless fingers occupied.

"Done," one of the women said in satisfaction. She sketched one last note on her clipboard with her black ballpoint pen and dropped it onto the table. "It should be done in a few days."

"That fast?" Cobalt said in surprise. "It would have taken the others, like, a week at least."

The blonde woman tapped her chin with a finger. "I'd like to see your saddle," she mused. "To see how we could improve."

"It's in the Loft with Alex's. Do you want me to bring it?"

She nodded enthusiastically, while the brunette looked on. "That'd be great."

I turned to lead him out, but the brunette grabbed my arm. I stiffened; so did Cobalt. The way my body was angled, he couldn't see what was wrong, but he knew something was. "I need to speak with you," she said in undertones.

I raised my voice a little. "It's fine, Cobalt. I'm sure Steel knows the way out?"

Yes, Steel confirmed. Cobalt followed him out, throwing worried glances over his shoulder like he couldn't figure out whether to intervene or not. I waved him out.

What's wrong? Stellar asked. I felt her surge to her feet, rustling her wings in irritation. *Do you need me to come?*

No, I responded, trying to keep my voice calm. I don't think she believed me, but she sank back down anyway.

"What?" I growled at the brunette. Her grip tightened on my arm, but the blonde put a hand on her arm to stop her.

"We just wanted to warn you," she began.

My strained temper frayed like a string pulled taut. I had been kidnapped and held captive for months, discovered an entirely different project with dragons, found out a long-held secret, and they thought it was the time to warn me about Cobalt?

"I've heard it all before," I spat. "I'm not going to desert him just because he has a questionable family background. Heck, I do too!"

The blonde's mouth quirked, then turned down, and she smiled sadly. "That's not what I was going to say."

"You weren't going to warn me about Cobalt, then?" I challenged. She flushed and tilted her head down. The brunette's grip tightened on my upper arm until I couldn't feel it anymore; I'd have a ring of bruises in the shape of her hand, I figured. I bruised easily, but it wouldn't be long.

"Not that kind of warning," she admitted.

I nodded, slightly mollified. "What were you going to say then?"

The sad smile returned. "I know his family. If you give one of them your heart, they'll keep it forever, or they'll shatter it into a thousand pieces."

I swallowed. I'd heard that kind of warning before, even given it a few times, but I had never really felt that it applied to anyone I knew. "How do you know them?"

She reached for the work table and grabbed a picture frame. I hadn't noticed it because I'd only been able to see the back. A view of cardboard and mahogany wasn't exactly going to hold my attention for long. When she turned it around, I gasped.

"No way."

Chapter Thirty-Eight

"Way," the blonde woman said.

The photo was of someone I knew: a slightly older Hale and a much younger blonde woman. They had their arms wrapped around each other, clearly in love, broad grins on their faces. Hale was older than the other photo; he also looked like he'd gotten over the junior professor look. He wore a leather aviator jacket and faded jeans, dark sunglasses shoved up into his hair, which was brown then.

"Did he dye his hair?" I wondered aloud. I realized too late that his hair shouldn't be what I was commenting on. Luckily, the woman understood, letting loose a ringing laugh. The brunette plopped me down on a stool, placing her hands on my shoulders and pressing down. I was too fascinated by the photo to feel more than a brief flash of irritation.

"No. When his dragon died, his aging sped up. In the span of a few months, he went from looking like a blonde teenager to a twenty-something brown haired guy. Within another six months, his hair was black and he looked several years older. It was great for disguises."

I frowned. "Who were you hiding from? I thought Hale said the scientists brought him back when he was knocked out and Sarja was killed."

She nodded. "They did. And he stayed, until he realized all they wanted him for was experiments." Her voice was bitter. "They wanted to know what would happen to a rider if their dragon died."

I winced. "So what happened? Also, what's your name? I can never keep you guys straight," I admitted sheepishly.

"I'm Andrea," the brunette inserted, while the blonde said, "I'm Tanya."

"Thanks," I said self-consciously. I fingered my necklace, which was spotted with fingerprints, and promised myself I would polish it later. It was my good luck talisman, and I rubbed it whenever I was thinking hard or felt unsafe. The women both nodded, broad grins on their faces despite my embarrassment. "So what happened?" I repeated.

Tanya sat on one of the rolling desk chairs and scooted it closer to my stool, on my right. Andrea did the same on my left, surrounding me. It made me uneasy, but I didn't think they realized what they were doing.

"He escaped. I was on a class trip in Europe when we met. I was eighteen and he looked like he was, oh, twenty-one or so. I had no way of telling he was actually my age."

"And you fell in love?" I probed wistfully.

She stared off into the distance, equally wistful. When Andrea poked her with a boot, she snapped out of it. "Yes," she answered. "We ran across Europe for months, trying to stay out of their reach."

"Why Europe?" I questioned. "Why not come back here?"

"Because we figured the scientists had no authority there. If they wanted him back, they'd have to kidnap him. That's illegal," she continued, stating the obvious.

"And they did anyway?" I guessed.

Another slow nod. "We went into town one day for a farmer's market." She stopped and swallowed, then reached for a tall bottle of water. She chugged several swallows and continued. "We didn't usually do things like that, but I convinced him it would be okay. Why did I do that?" she trailed off. Another irritated poke from Andrea, who looked like she thought Tanya was taking too long.

"Get to the point," she chided. "The poor girl's gonna die of boredom pretty soon."

I laughed; mine wasn't nearly as clear as Tanya's earlier one had been. My voice was deeper when I spoke, so my laugh was deeper and sounded like a clock's chime. So had Tanya's, but hers had been more bell than clock. "I'm fascinated," I admitted. "I'm perfectly content to sit here and listen to her story all day. I've got nothing better to do."

"Didn't David tell you to restart your training?" Andrea asked suspiciously.

"Did he?" I asked, falsely innocent. I all but batted my eyelashes. She burst out laughing and dropped it with a wave of her hand, her mouth twisted up in a half smile.

"Anyhow," Tanya grumped. "We were in the market, and I turned my back for two minutes, tops. When I turned back around, he was gone. I didn't even hear him yell, although he claims he did."

I reached out and touched her arm gently. "I'm sorry. What did you do after that?"

"I flew back home," she said instantly. "I searched for him for weeks. Weeks turned into months, months turned into years."

"What did you tell your parents?" I asked curiously. My parents would have dragged me back in chains if I'd gone wandering for that long, especially if they found out it was related to a boy.

She gave an unladylike snort. Not that she was a priss, but she was more of a lady than Andrea, who sat with her legs splayed, picking at her fingernails with one of the awls they used to carve the leather. "My parents fancied themselves responsible, but they wanted me to be able to make my own choices, or so they said. I think they just didn't care. At first they checked in every few months, but eventually they just gave up and washed their hands of me. I was always the black sheep of the family," she said proudly. I knew all about that. My parents were both from well-to-do families who couldn't be prouder of their doctor children. When the secret of dragons came out, I couldn't wait to see their expressions. I rubbed my palms together lightly in anticipation just thinking about it.

"So how did you find him?" I asked, leaning forward and propping my elbows on my knees, unconsciously mimicking Andrea's pose. I realized it after a second and just as quickly decided I didn't care enough to move.

Tanya's eyes were starry with remembrance. "It took me three years. I finally found him, but only because of Micah." Her voice was sour and reluctant; she clearly didn't want to admit what she owed Micah. "He'd killed every one of the scientists, including his father." She took a shaky breath, hugging herself as she relived the memory; Andrea leaned over and wrapped her arm around her friend's shoulders. "When I arrived, Hale was strapped to a table and unconscious. I dragged him out of there. I knew who had done it, and I was terrified. For both of us."

My hand was clamped over my mouth, my palm dusted with each shallow exhalation. I couldn't believe Hale was still sane after something like that. He had a reason to be insane, but wasn't; what was Micah's excuse? "So Hale and Micah's father was one of the scientists?"

This time Andrea answered. "Yes. And I believe he was your boy's father, as well?"

I shook my head. I didn't even bother denying that Cobalt was "my boy". I was no longer even sure that he wasn't. "They have the same mother, not father."

"How do you know?"

"Micah made a crack," I growled. She nodded understandingly.

I sat bolt upright and face-palmed. "Oh, geez," I breathed. "He's probably lost in another supply closet."

Identical raised brows, but neither of the women commented. "You're welcome here anytime," Tanya offered. To my surprise, Andrea nodded, far more enthusiastically than I would have expected from someone so reserved.

"Thanks," I said, already headed for the door. "Cobalt, where are you?"

Chapter Thirty-Nine

"What's going on?" I asked outside. Cobalt leaned against Steel's chest; his saddle was in his lap. Stellar rested her head on Steel's back, just behind his neck; she looked like she was asleep.

"Nothing," Cobalt said nonchalantly. I didn't trust it. His eyes had met mine and then skittered away, a clear sign that someone knows what people look for in a liar and are trying to fool. I opened my mouth to respond, but Cobalt shoved to his feet. "I need to take this in to them," he said.

What's going on? I asked Stellar suspiciously. She lifted her broad shoulders and rustled her wings, the dragon equivalent of a shrug.

I don't know. She fell silent for a minute, and then said, *Steel would like to speak to you. May he?*

I blinked in surprise. *Sure.*

I would prefer he tell you himself, and I will attempt to get him to do so, but if he does not, I will tell you.

Tell me what?

Wait.

I crossed my arms and waited impatiently. It took ten minutes for Cobalt to return. "What's going on?" I barked without preamble.

His face closed. "I don't know what you're talking about," he lied.

"Your dragon sold you out," I said flatly. "Share."

He flopped down dramatically, shooting a filthy glare at Steel, but he was smart enough to know that between his dragon and a woman, there was no possible way he was going to win this argument. "I was listening to you guys," he admitted. "I never knew that about my brother. Either of them," he added.

I swallowed hard. "How much did you hear?" I asked feebly. If he heard the whole conversation, not only did he hear Tanya's warning (embarrassing!), he would have also heard that one brother had been kidnapped and one had killed his own father.

"All of it," he said grimly. "I shouldn't have listened. I wish I hadn't."

I scooted over and laid my head on his shoulder. By now, both dragons were asleep. We were around the corner of the building, so I wasn't worried about someone seeing us. "When the dragons wake up, do you want to go for a flight?"

He nodded enthusiastically. "Definitely. But I'm supposed to speak with David."

I pointed, explaining the directions slowly and carefully. "I'll be back," he said, smacking an exaggerated kiss on my cheek. I waved goodbye and closed my eyes. If the dragons were having a nap, why couldn't I?

"What are you doing?"

I jerked awake, reaching reflexively for my dagger and finding an empty sheath. I had forgotten to ask Ice to return it; it was still back at the Base, which left me without a weapon.

"Yes, Chase?" I said, struggling to keep my cool. It was rude to wake anyone, doubly so for dragons and riders. We don't sleep a lot to begin with; we have to have at least some, which is why we nap so much. Dragons just do it because they feel like it.

"I feel badly for how I treated you before you left," he said. "I wanted to apologize." I racked my brain for a specific instance. I mean, sure, he'd been rude and arrogant, but that wasn't a change. Besides, he didn't seem like the type to apologize for it.

"There's no need," I said slowly. He waved his hand.

"There is every need. I was rude; my behavior was inexcusable." He reached into his breast pocket and pulled something out; it glittered in his palm. "I found this. It reminded me of you. I want you to have it."

He extended his hand; I took it from him slowly. It was a tungsten ring, colored smoky black. An elaborate fleur-de-lis was imposed on the stone in sapphires, standing out starkly.

"Thank you," I said. I slid the ring onto my right ring finger; it fit perfectly.

"I'm glad it fits," he said in satisfaction. "I wasn't sure it would."

When he walked away, I pulled my necklace out of my shirt. I hadn't worn so much jewelry in my entire life. They didn't clash horribly, not that I would have cared if they did.

I still couldn't wrap my head around the fact that Chase had given me a gift. Weird.

Chapter Forty

"What's that?" Cobalt asked.

"What's what?" I frowned.

He pointed at the ring gracing my right hand. "Chase gave it to me."

"Why?"

I shrugged eloquently. "Dunno. Anyway, any thoughts on how we can find the mole?"

He shook his head in frustration. "No, none. I just can't think of anything."

"Me neither. I guess we'll just have to eliminate people one at a time."

"Which will take forever," he finished; I nodded glumly.

We sat in the Loft that night after dinner, on my platform. We didn't have enough space for all the new riders coming in, so I had agreed to let Cobalt stay with me. It was actually a bit of a tight squeeze, with two dragons, two riders, and a cot all crammed onto a narrow shelf.

I'd beggared a thick yellow notepad from the house, along with a pen, and we were in business. Cobalt and I had made a list of every rider whose name we knew (i.e. I knew). We'd begun to cross them off one by one, through the process of asking nonchalant questions about their whereabouts and then checking up on their stories. So far, the amount of people crossed off was depressingly small, the list still to be determined disheartening large.

Actually, we'd only managed to cross off three riders; all who had been in separate areas at the time we suspected the information had been passed. I'd argued that Meisha and Orion should be crossed off, but Cobalt had rebutted that we didn't know their whereabouts, not for sure. This was going to take longer than I had thought, longer than we had. Time was of the essence.

It had been weeks since we'd returned, with frustratingly little to show for all of our work. Cobalt and I had begun taking long flights together. Others teased us mercilessly, but it was really just an excuse to work on our list. The amount of black scratches on the page was slowly growing, but too slowly for my taste.

Both projects were doing well, despite having a traitor in our midst. Nearly all of the riders from The Base had joined us. Hale had to organize strategic missions so that riders were out at the right time, since we didn't have enough room. Tanya and Andrea were hard at work providing newer and better saddles for The Base riders; Madame LaVarne spent practically all of her time in her workshop to provide new and improved uniforms for them, as well as for the new riders who would soon be arriving. I wouldn't have been surprised if she slept in that room, on a nest of fabrics.

I had to help with the workout schedule, as well as anything else I wanted to. I was climbing the walls, being the only rider not sent out on missions. Even Cobalt was sent out; he grimaced apologetically at me and gave me a light kiss each time Steel took flight and we were left grounded. I helped the women with the saddles: my limited sewing knowledge was good enough for Madame LaVarne.

I sighed and stretched out on the platform. A sudden inrush of missions had left the barn practically empty, except for us. Stellar didn't have nearly the problem I did with being held back. She enjoyed the long naps and equally long flights. It had been a long day with Madame LaVarne. I had never seen so many sequins in my entire life. My fingers ached from the needle.

Claws clicked on my platform. I sat bolt upright, fumbling for the electric LED lantern that sat on my abandoned cot. A soft chirp sounded from somewhere near my knee cap, and the light blared on. A tiny dragon chittered happily, swishing her wings and puffing her chest out importantly. A tiny leather collar was wrapped around her neck; the front bulged strangely.

Stellar lifted her head curiously, touching muzzles with the smaller dragon. Apparently having decided it wasn't worth her time, she licked my arm and laid back down.

I reached out my hand to stroke the little one and she leaned into it like a cat, humming deep in her chest. "What are you doing here?" I wondered aloud, even though I had a good idea. She wiggled a little while I tried to figure out how to open the flap at the front of her collar, but I finally succeeded, rewarded with a stately piece of tan stationary. It had been folded into tiny pieces until it had fit into the collar.

"Good girl," I praised; she bowed, forelegs on the ground and butt in the air, like a dog's play bow. Her wings fluttered as she took flight, leaving me to read the note in the glaringly bright light of the lantern.

Alex,

It has recently come to my attention that you have been privy to information about my past. I trust you, and you seem to mean a lot to my younger brother, so I would like to further explain the happenings in my past. Please come to my office as soon as you are available. I would like to reduce the risk of us being overheard.

Hale

Stellar finally stirred, lifting her head and exhaling her warm breath over my back as she read the note over my shoulder. Dragons could read if their riders could, but couldn't write, because their claws wouldn't allow it. Since dragons shared our minds, they learned human skills like speaking and reading by observation. Often they don't know what words mean, but they can use them in correct context because they heard it somewhere else first.

You should go. She heaved herself to her feet and fluttered her wings, anxious to get this over with so she could go back to sleep. I sprang onto her shoulders, twisting so I didn't impale myself on her maze of neck and back spikes.

Once you take me down, I'll walk. When I need to get back up, I'll wake you, I promised. She huffed in agreement and swooped silently toward the ground, flaring her wings out at the last second with a twang like a flicked rubber band. Her hind legs hit the ground first, powerful thigh muscles straining; her front paws settled onto the ground with a click of claws. I placed my palms on her neck and pushed up, swinging out and over her spikes.

Go back to bed, I sent fondly. *Before you go, what time is it?*

Two thirty-one a.m., was the immediate response. For some reason, dragons always knew what time it was, which meant I didn't have to wear a watch to know the time. She bumped my shoulder with her head and snaked her tail around my ankles for a second before she was up again.

It was a long walk to the house. I swept my flashlight across the long grass, searching for any holes or large rocks to trip over. I hadn't taken my jewelry off before I went to bed, so my necklace clinked gently against my chest as I walked. My right ring finger itched; I shifted the ring so I could scratch it. The skin felt odd, but it was probably just my imagination. I couldn't see anything in the darkness. I'd worry about it later.

A shape reared up in front of me. I reached instinctively for my dagger, once again forgetting that Ice still had it, back at The Base. *I really need to get that back*, I thought offhandedly.

The snake flicked its tongue, unimpressed, then lowered itself to the ground and slithered away. Actually, right over the toe of my boot; I twitched. I wasn't afraid of snakes, but the very thought of them touching me, even my boot, made me cringe. It was ironic, considering that I shared my mind, and everything else, with a dragon. She wouldn't have liked to hear this, but Stellar was basically just an enormous snake with wings.

I trudged up the steps and onto the porch. It wrapped almost entirely around the house; it was an uncomfortable place to be in the dark, all those hiding places. I'm sure it's not just me, but I become a lot more paranoid in the dark. Too many horror movies, I guess. That's what I get for hanging out with guys almost my entire life.

The lights in the house were on, but dimmed to their lowest setting. The plush carpeting sprang under my feet as I walked slowly up the hallway. The game room was silent and dark; I didn't think I'd ever seen the flat screen TV in the center turned off. The kitchen was dark as well; the checkered black and white tiles were intermittent flashes of light and darkness.

I knocked lightly on Hale's door. It struck me as kind of redundant; there probably weren't too many people around the house at three o'clock in the morning.

Hale called for me to come in. I pushed the door open slowly, startled when it squeaked harshly. It hadn't done that before.

"What are you doing up this early, sir?" I asked. Two steps in and I seated myself in the high backed leather chair across his desk. He looked haggard, his gray hair limp and face drooping. His eyes had thick bags under them; I was worried for him.

"This was important," he said gravely. "I needed to speak with you immediately."

"About what, sir? I'm sure nostalgia stories could have waited a few more hours." Maybe not as delicate or tactful as I could have put it, but I was not a morning person. I couldn't be expected to function properly, which included manners.

He waved his hand dismissively. "We'll talk about that later. Right now, we have something more to talk about."

"Like what?" I repeated. Looks like I wasn't the only one who couldn't function properly. What was with all the lead-up, anyway?

"You know that we have a traitor in our midst," he began solemnly.

"Have you figured out who it is?" I asked excitedly. My bony elbows dug into the top of my knees as I leaned forward with rapt attention.

He hesitated. "Perhaps," he said mysteriously. "But we have a bigger problem at hand, closely related to the mole. My brother has escaped."

I choked. "Sir?!" I blurted, my voice rising in pitch.

News flash: while we teenagers, the ones who had actually apprehended him, couldn't decide what to do with Micah, his twin had no such qualms. A few covert calls later, Micah had been packed off in an anonymous white van with no markings or license plate, by men in jumpsuits. They wore dark sunglasses and refused to speak to us when we addressed them, no matter how much we pestered. We still didn't know where Micah's dragon was, a small problem that I had tried to ignore. One issue at a time.

"We believe his accomplice helped to orchestrate it," Hale said grimly.

"You give me too much credit," a voice said, falsely modest. Bright light flared; I flinched and threw my hand up to shield my face. Like I said, photosensitive, not that anyone reacts well to a having a light shone in their eyes.

"Chase?" Hale said in confusion. "What are you talking about?"

"You never even suspected me, did you?" Chase said smugly. He wore a gray leather duster, layered over a beige sweater and tan cargo pants. His long blonde hair had been trimmed neatly, an almost military look. It reminded me disturbingly of General Mafector, another nutter who had disappeared in the move.

"I did, actually," I sneered coolly. "I knew there was a reason I didn't like you."

He sneered back. "One of my biggest flaws is impatience. Micah told me how to kill you, helped me even, but I'm not patient enough to wait."

I went cold. What did he mean, wait? Had he already done something to try and kill me? "What are you talking about?"

"How do you like your ring?" he asked innocently.

I reached for the ring, trying to tamp down my panic. I twisted it off my finger, revealing ugly, puckered skin. It was too dark, an unhealthy color. "What did you do to me?"

"Belladonna was a drug used, ages ago, as a fashion statement. Women would use it to make their eyes large and luminous," he narrated.

I was thrown. I was prepared for a lot of things with a crazy traitor, but a history lesson was not one of them. "That's all fascinating, but what does it have to do with me?"

"What they didn't realize," he continued, "was that in large quantities, it could kill you. A deadly poison, used as a means of making one more beautiful. Ironic, really, considering how sick it could make them."

"Then why aren't I sick?" I challenged. "I feel perfectly fine."

He huffed. "That's where my impatience comes in. I was supposed to give you the ring, get out of here before anyone realized something was wrong, but here's a secret: I never liked you either." He produced a gun from the pocket of the duster, leveling it at my chest. "I'll kill you first, then Hale. Save Micah some time, you know," he said conversationally.

"Go ahead," I dared.

I had never been a good card player. At first I was too cautious, refusing to take any chances. Then I was too bold, taking chances I couldn't afford if someone called my bluff. I had never grown out of that too-bold phase.

"Okay," he said agreeably, and pulled the trigger. Something hit my chest, near my heart; the floor rushed up to meet me like a soft pillow after a hard day.

Epilogue

I felt like the elephant in the room was seated on my chest. I struggled to breathe; my eyes were closed tightly to keep the bright light from filtering in.

Someone shook my shoulder. I wanted to tell them to knock it off, that it hurt, but I couldn't muster the energy.

"Alex? Can you hear me?" a voice asked, sounding like it was struggling not to panic.

I can hear you, I grumped. *I just don't care.*

That's hardly the attitude to have, Stellar chided, sounding immensely relieved.

A brief silence, then the voice said, "I know you're awake. Can you open your eyes, please?"

Tattle tale.

He was worried about you, she defended.

Who? Hale?

Try again.

I am not going to play a guessing game, I warned. I coughed; deep hacks, still struggling to breathe. The pressure eased slowly.

Open your eyes.

Fine! Stubborn as ever, I waited a minute to open my eyes. When I finally did, a familiar face swam into view. It took several rapid blinks to bring my vision into focus, but I would have known that face in a crowd of a thousand. Blurry, teared vision wasn't enough.

Cobalt sighed in relief and rocked back onto his heels. "She's fine," he assured someone, just out of my vision. I started to roll my head to see; a jagged throb of pain stopped me quick.

Cobalt glanced down, a worried frown drawing his eyebrows together. "You are okay, right?" he checked.

A delicate throat clearing. "I think the medics should make that assessment," a stately voice chided. Must be Hale. No one else I know sounds that classy.

I placed my palms on the ground and levered myself slowly to a sitting position, staunchly ignoring various outspoken protests.

"Where was I shot?" I asked quietly; my throat scraped.

Cobalt crossed his legs, seeming perfectly content to sit on the hard floor as long as I did. He tapped his chest, about an inch to the left of his collarbone. "You see, that's the thing," he began.

"What?" I asked, voice rising in panic. "What happened?"

"Nothing bad," Hale promised. He leaned forward from the chair he'd pulled up, knees creaking, and patted my shoulder soothingly. "In fact, it was quite lucky."

I peeled down my shirt and stared. My necklace, which I wore so often I didn't even notice it anymore, was gone. The skin where it usually sat was red and inflamed, twisted like the birthmark on my hip. No blood, no nothing.

Cobalt held something out to me, opening his palm. I took it from him, not minding that our hands brushed, and studied the item he'd given me. My necklace hung dented, just barely on the chain, missing links. The center, with my initials, was bent back; it produced a sort of miniature bowl, the kind a new-to-pottery worker would make. My eyes teared up a little at seeing it nearly destroyed, but I was sure the boys would be glad to hear that their gift had saved my life, if I ever got the chance to contact them again. I'd have it repaired as soon as possible, but I shuddered to think what could have happened if it had been made of a cheap material, rather than high-quality silver.

I soaked in my surroundings, trying to ignore the throbbing in my chest, near my heart. The sharp edge of my necklace dug into my hand as I looked around. Cobalt sat across from me, knees crossed; his black hair stuck up in all directions, like he'd run his hands through it again and again. His blue eyes had bags beneath them. I hadn't noticed before, but a frying pan sat on the ground next to his thigh.

I arched my brows and stared pointedly at the pan. Cobalt got the hint immediately. "I walked in on you guys just as Chase shot you. I grabbed the nearest thing that could be a weapon and hit him over the head with it. I'm just lucky it was a pan and not, like, a banana," he added, mouth twisting in a wry, self-deprecating grin.

"And I'm just lucky you came back from your mission so soon," I mused. "So what are we going to do with him?"

Orion and Meisha, seated side by side on the edge of the couch, shared Cobalt's expression of disdain. I was sure the others would hear about this soon.

"Unlike my brother," the same disdainful expression as the others, "we can get charges against him to stick. We have proof and very good lawyers. He will go to jail," Hale vowed.

"But we have a problem," Meisha said hesitantly.

My eyes rolled of their own volition. "Of course there is," I said, my voice thick with sarcasm and exasperation.

Meisha smiled grimly, obviously of the same opinion. "Chase's dragon escaped before we knew. We couldn't get there in time to stop him."

I understood the problem immediately; my empathetic groan racked my already pained chest. "And he's most likely already met up with Micah. They're probably plotting how best to break Chase out at this very moment."

Orion waited for that to sink in before he piped up. "And that's not even the worst part."

I couldn't help it. I groaned and dropped my head into my hands, which didn't help my headache or my chest. I held up one finger in the universal just-a-minute sign; something shuffled.

A warm palm rested on my back, massaging in slow circles. I kept my head in my hands for a minute longer, basking in relief.

When I looked up, Cobalt was the only one in the room with me. The others had cleared out quickly; the couch was as empty as Roanoke colony, cushions still depressed.

"They bailed," I observed, massaging my temple. Cobalt took over almost immediately, his long fingers wrinkling and smoothing my skin.

"They thought it might be better if we had a moment alone," he explained.

"They stuck you with explaining the problem, didn't they?" I guessed. He grimaced.

"Right."

I sighed gustily. "What is it?"

"They found a note while they were looking through Micah's things," he said slowly.

I went cold. "What did they find?" I asked, enunciating clearly.

"Proof that we aren't the only dragon projects. For years, he's been funneling riders with... how should I put this... loose morals, to another property."

"His own personal army," I breathed. It was even worse than I'd thought. "So he'll come after us when Chase's dragon tells him Chase got caught."

He nodded grimly, dark hair sliding over his forehead and into his eyes. "We sent riders after the dragon, but we ..."

"Don't have high hopes," I finished glumly. "This is so bad. Do we know anything more?"

He shook his head, mouth tightening into a straight line. "Hale didn't say anything, but he was worried. I've got a bad feeling about this."

"Me too," I agreed offhandedly. My mind churned with ideas and plans. "Will you give me a few minutes alone? I need to go see Stellar."

"Of course," he said immediately. He kissed my cheek lightly and walked out, turning into the kitchen. I followed him, striding slowly to the door and trying to lose the feeling that my head was going to roll off of my shoulders.

Stellar swooped toward me, trumpeting. *Stop that,* I ordered. *My head hurts enough already.*

Sorry. She angled her wings and lowered her hind legs smoothly, rocking forward onto her forelegs. She buried her muzzle in my chest, and I yelped when she brushed the tender skin. She ripped her nose away, licking it gently in apology. *Does it hurt?*

Yes.

I'm sorry.

I sank to the ground, wrapping my arms around my knees and leaning back. *What will we do? If dragons fight, we'll have lost the chance to introduce them to the world. Who knew what would happen?*

You're afraid. It was such a candid observation that my eyes filled with tears. I wasn't just afraid; I was terrified. If dragons and their riders went to war, an extinct species revived would become extinct again. If I lost Stellar, I'd go insane.

Or, what if the world didn't react well to being kept out of the loop? I knew I wouldn't react well. Nonetheless, it brought to mind horrific visions of government experiments and angry, chanting mobs. What would we do?

"You're worried," Cobalt observed. He peeked around the corner. Steel popped up behind him, just above his head. He put his back against the wall and slid down next to me.

I nodded in agreement, still furiously blinking back tears. Without another word, he opened his arm, and I scooted into the curve of his side, breathing in his musky smell. "Don't be," he said, burying his nose in my hair, which was falling down from its braid. He twisted a strand around his finger as we sat.

I turned my face turned him and kissed him gently. My mouth tasted like salt and rust; I'd bitten my lip earlier. I started to pull away, but he shifted with me. There was an irrational surge of jealousy for something ridiculous: his eyelashes. They were so long they brushed my cheekbones, making me smile against his warm lips. My hand rested lightly on his back, where it stayed until he finally broke away.

We leaned back, flat against the wall, panting. After a few minutes, he leaned forward and pulled something from behind his back. It glinted on his palm.

"My dagger," I said, irrationally happy about such a small thing. I fitted it carefully back into its empty sheath, which had hung on my hip this whole time.

"I was bringing it to you when I walked in," he explained shyly. He ran his fingers through his thick hair yet again, making it stick up even further.

"At three o'clock in the morning?"

"I knew you wanted it back," he mumbled, flushed bright red. He fiddled with a strand of his own hair and refused to make eye contact.

I kissed him again, a surprise brush of lips. "That is amazing," I said fervently. As I leaned back and studied him, I was struck at the rightness of it. I was surrounded by dragons, the most amazing creatures you could think of. I had great friends, with the prospect of many more to come as the two projects converged. And Cobalt, a great friend who had the potential to be far more.

Yeah, maybe we had our problems. The two groups would clash for a while, I imagined. My friends had their moments, but I'd never been that great at making friends; I had no reason to think that would change now. I wasn't at all sure what to do with Cobalt, but I was sure that he would be around until I decided. And the biggest problem of all: our dragons. Would we be able to reveal their existence to the world at large as we'd planned? Or would we go to war, risking the lives of everyone I knew and cared about? I didn't know, but I did know this: whatever happened, we'd be right at the center of it.

About the Author

Julie Kramer is a debut author who lives in Ohio. She is taking college classes, and often uses writing her next book as an excuse not to do homework. The books that she writes are various types of fantasy, with lots of action and just a smidgen of romance. She loves hearing from readers. Check out her next book, if you please!

APR 1 3 2018

Made in the USA
San Bernardino, CA
06 April 2018